D1360843

A STORY OF MEN

ZEP

ISBN: 978-1-63140-961-5   20 19 18 17   1 2 3 4

A STORY OF MEN. FIRST PRINTING. SEPTEMBER 2017. Translation
and Lettering © 2017 IDW Publishing. Story and Art © 2017 Rue de
Sevres. All Rights Reserved. IDW Publishing, a division of Idea and
Design Works, LLC. Editorial offices: 2765 Truxtun Road, San Diego,
CA 92106. Any similarities to persons living or dead are purely
coincidental. With the exception of artwork used for review purposes,
none of the contents of this publication may be reprinted without
the permission of Idea and Design Works, LLC. Printed in Korea.

IDW Publishing does not read or accept unsolicited submissions
of ideas, stories, or artwork.

Ted Adams, CEO & Publisher
Greg Goldstein, President & COO
Robbie Robbins, EVP/Sr. Graphic Artist
Chris Ryall, Chief Creative Officer
David Hedgecock, Editor-in-Chief
Laurie Windrow, Senior VP of Sales & Marketing
Matthew Ruzicka, CPA, Chief Financial Officer
Lorelei Bunjes, VP of Digital Services
Jerry Bennington, VP of New Product Development

For international rights, please
contact licensing@idwpublishing.com

First published in France as *Une histoire d'hommes*
© 2013 Rue de Sèvres, Paris.

Written and Illustrated by **Zep**

Lettered by **Frank Cvetkovic**

Translated by **Ivanka Hahnenberger**

Edited by **Justin Eisinger**

Production Design by **Ron Estevez**

Publisher: **Ted Adams**

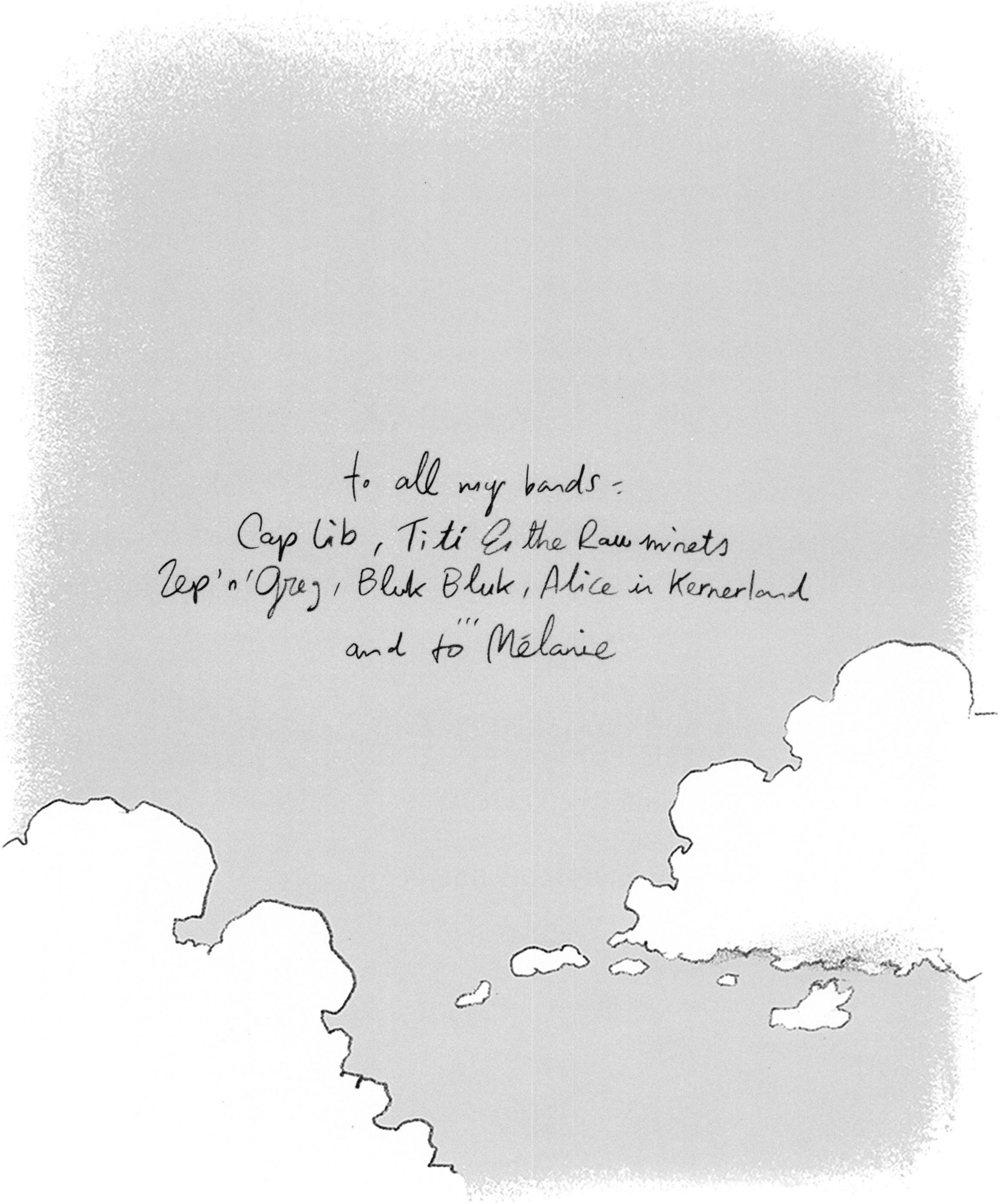
to all my bands :
Cap Lib, Titi & the Raw minets
Zep'n'Greg, Bluk Bluk, Alice in Kernerland
and to Mélanie

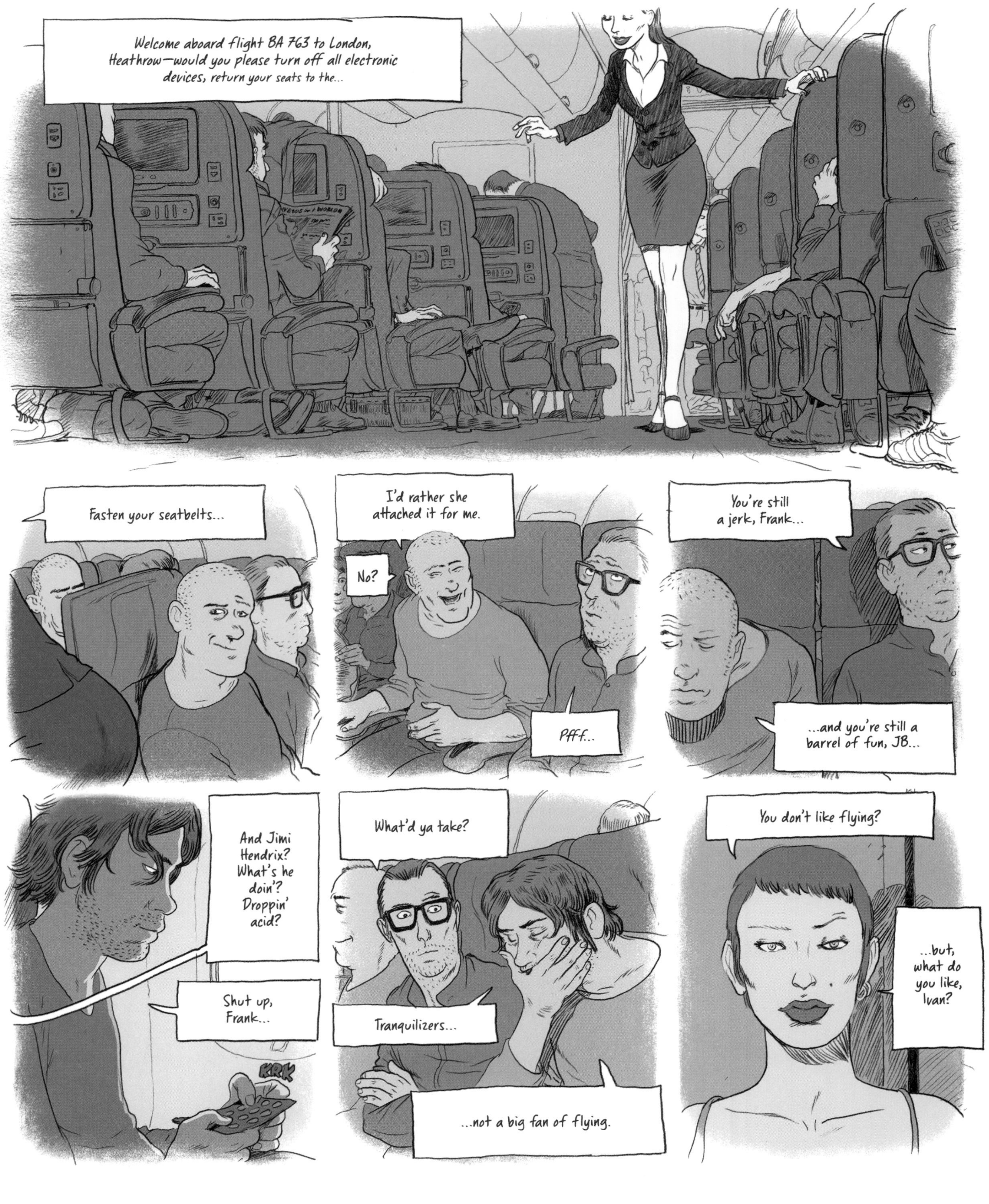
Welcome aboard flight BA 763 to London, Heathrow—would you please turn off all electronic devices, return your seats to the...
Fasten your seatbelts...
I'd rather she attached it for me.
No?
Pfff...
You're still a jerk, Frank...
...and you're still a barrel of fun, JB...
And Jimi Hendrix? What's he doin'? Droppin' acid?
Shut up, Frank...
KRIK
What'd ya take?
Tranquilizers...
...not a big fan of flying.
You don't like flying?
...but, what do you like, Ivan?

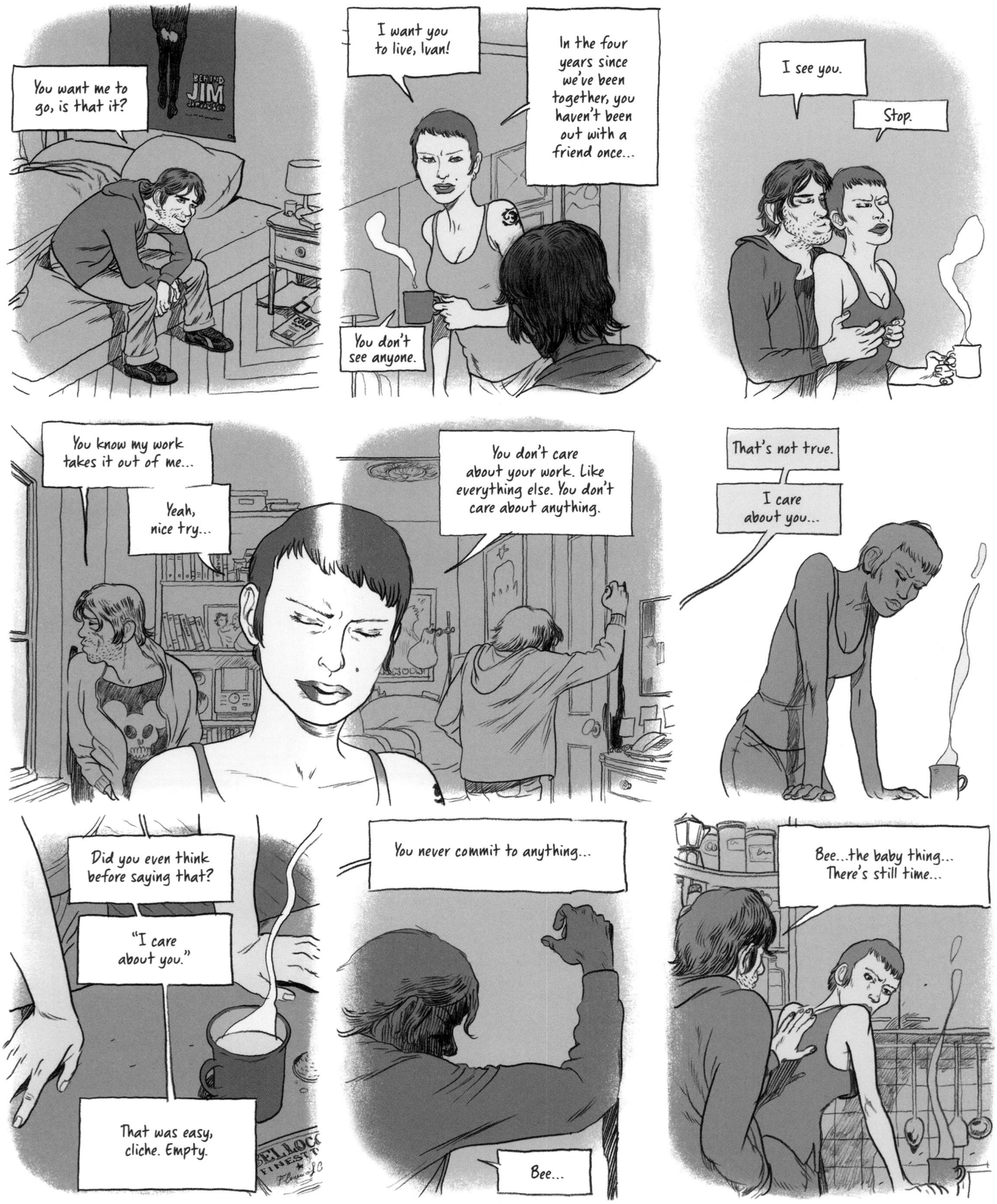

You want me to go, is that it?
BEHIND JIM
I want you to live, Ivan!
In the four years since we've been together, you haven't been out with a friend once...
You don't see anyone.
I see you.
Stop.
You know my work takes it out of me...
Yeah, nice try...
You don't care about your work. Like everything else. You don't care about anything.
That's not true.
I care about you...
Did you even think before saying that?
"I care about you."
That was easy, cliche. Empty.
You never commit to anything...
Bee...
Bee...the baby thing... There's still time...

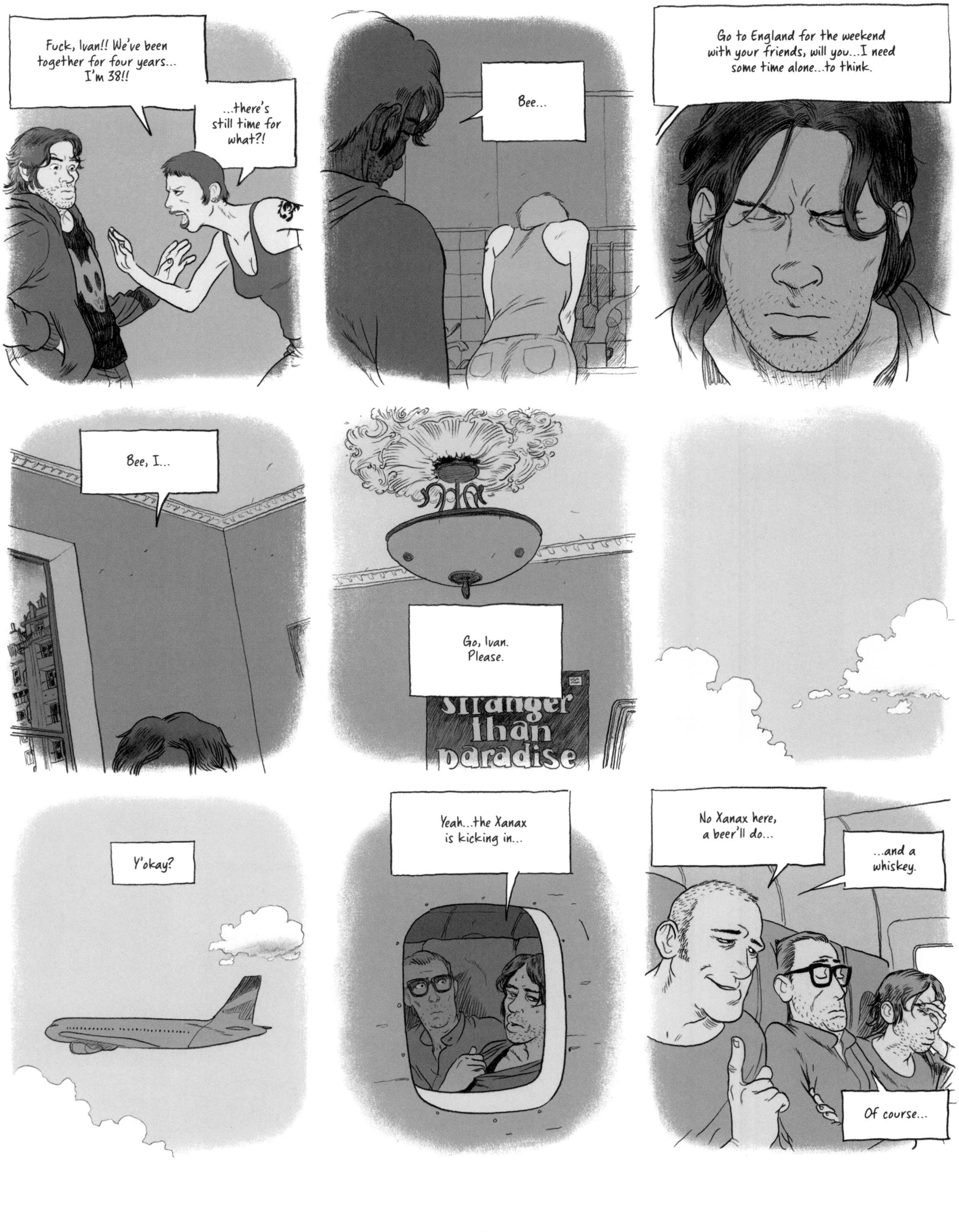
Fuck, Ivan!! We've been together for four years... I'm 38!!
...there's still time for what?!
Bee...
Go to England for the weekend with your friends, will you...I need some time alone...to think.
Bee, I...
Go, Ivan. Please.
Stranger than paradise
Y'okay?
Yeah...the Xanax is kicking in...
No Xanax here, a beer'll do...
...and a whiskey.
Of course...

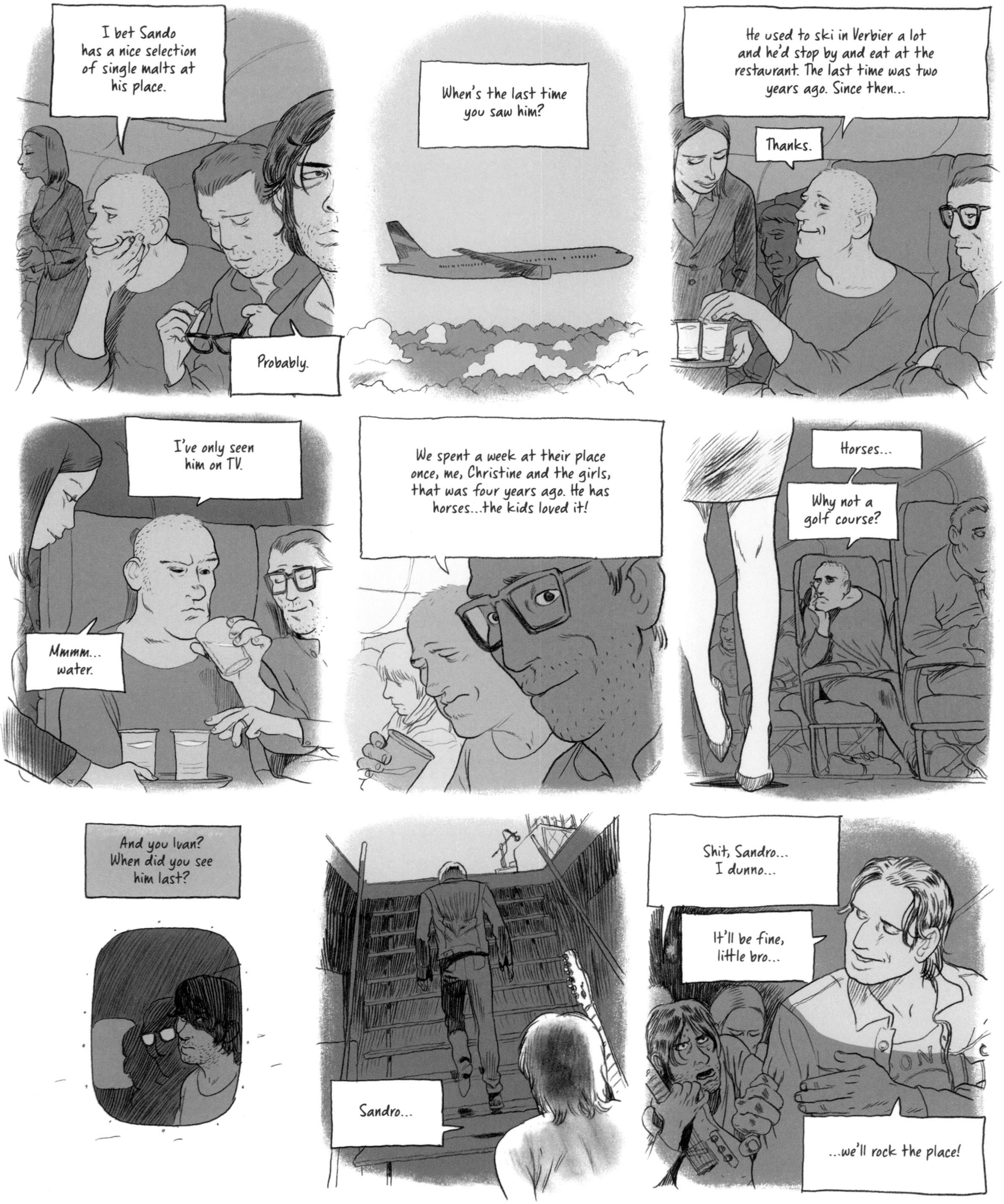
I bet Sando has a nice selection of single malts at his place.
Probably.
When's the last time you saw him?
He used to ski in Verbier a lot and he'd stop by and eat at the restaurant. The last time was two years ago. Since then...
Thanks.
I've only seen him on TV.
Mmmm... water.
We spent a week at their place once, me, Christine and the girls, that was four years ago. He has horses...the kids loved it!
Horses...
Why not a golf course?
And you Ivan? When did you see him last?
Sandro...
Shit, Sandro... I dunno...
It'll be fine, little bro...
...we'll rock the place!

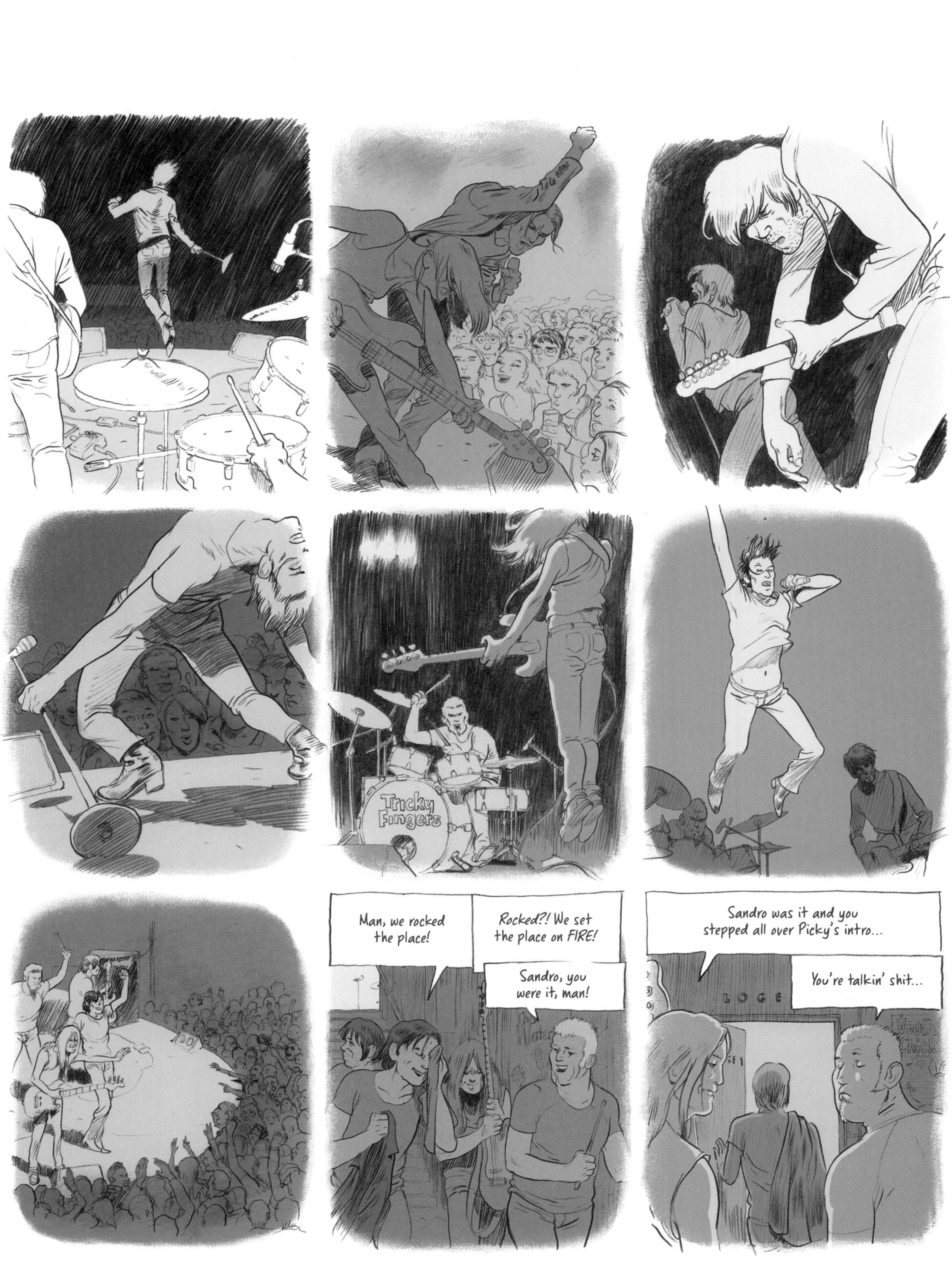
Tricky Fingers
Man, we rocked the place!
Rocked?! We set the place on FIRE!
Sandro, you were it, man!
Sandro was it and you stepped all over Picky's intro...
You're talkin' shit...
LOGE

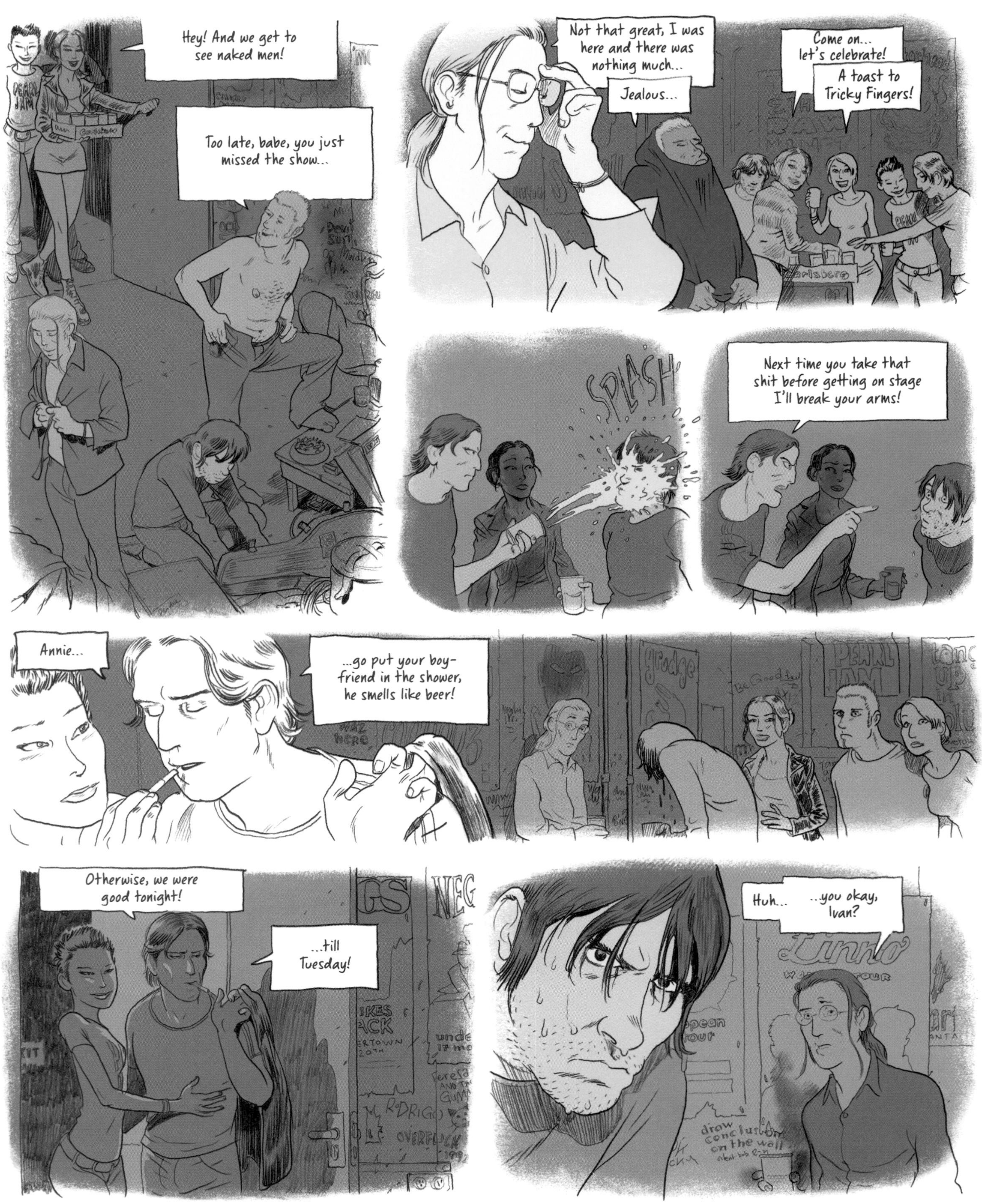
Hey! And we get to see naked men!
Too late, babe, you just missed the show...
Not that great, I was here and there was nothing much...
Jealous...
Come on... let's celebrate!
A toast to Tricky Fingers!
SPLASH!
Next time you take that shit before getting on stage I'll break your arms!
Annie...
...go put your boy-friend in the shower, he smells like beer!
Otherwise, we were good tonight!
...till Tuesday!
Huh...
...you okay, Ivan?

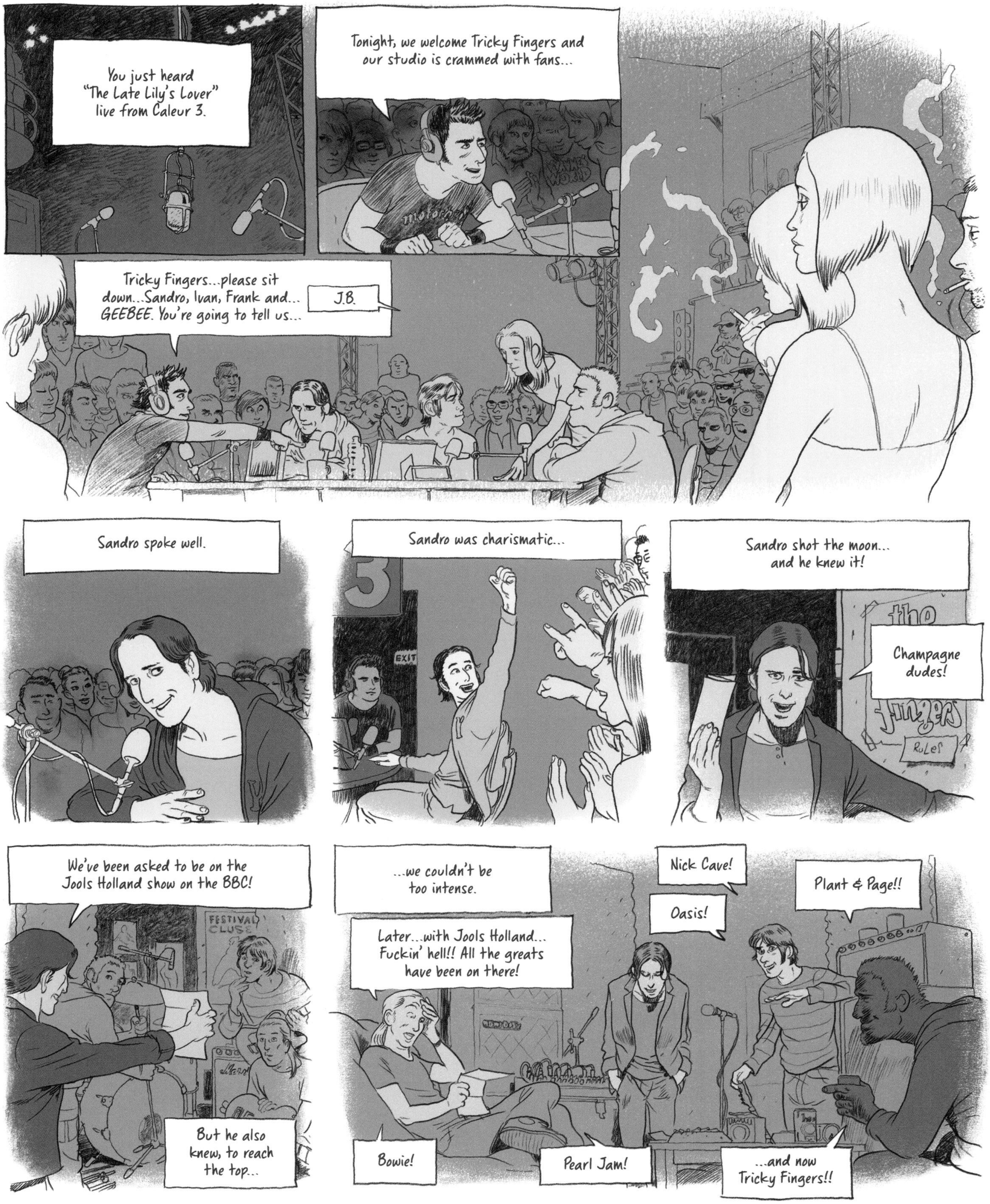

You just heard "The Late Lily's Lover" live from Caleur 3.
Tonight, we welcome Tricky Fingers and our studio is crammed with fans...
Tricky Fingers...please sit down...Sandro, Ivan, Frank and... GEEBEE. You're going to tell us...
J.B.
Sandro spoke well.
Sandro was charismatic...
Sandro shot the moon... and he knew it!
Champagne dudes!
We've been asked to be on the Jools Holland show on the BBC!
But he also knew, to reach the top...
...we couldn't be too intense.
Later...with Jools Holland... Fuckin' hell!! All the greats have been on there!
Nick Cave!
Oasis!
Plant & Page!!
Bowie!
Pearl Jam!
...and now Tricky Fingers!!

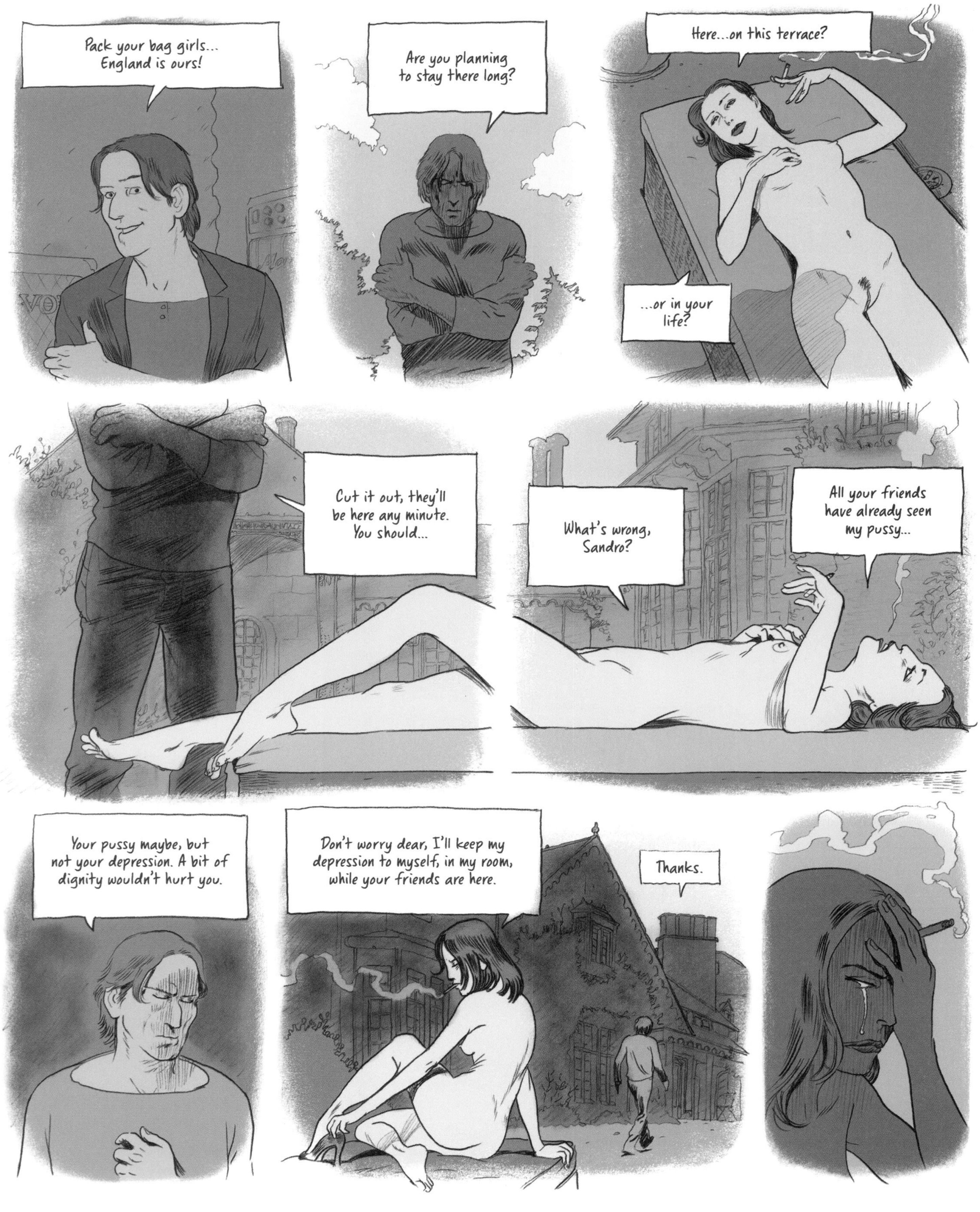
Pack your bag girls... England is ours!
Are you planning to stay there long?
Here...on this terrace?
...or in your life?
Cut it out, they'll be here any minute. You should...
What's wrong, Sandro?
All your friends have already seen my pussy...
Your pussy maybe, but not your depression. A bit of dignity wouldn't hurt you.
Don't worry dear, I'll keep my depression to myself, in my room, while your friends are here.
Thanks.

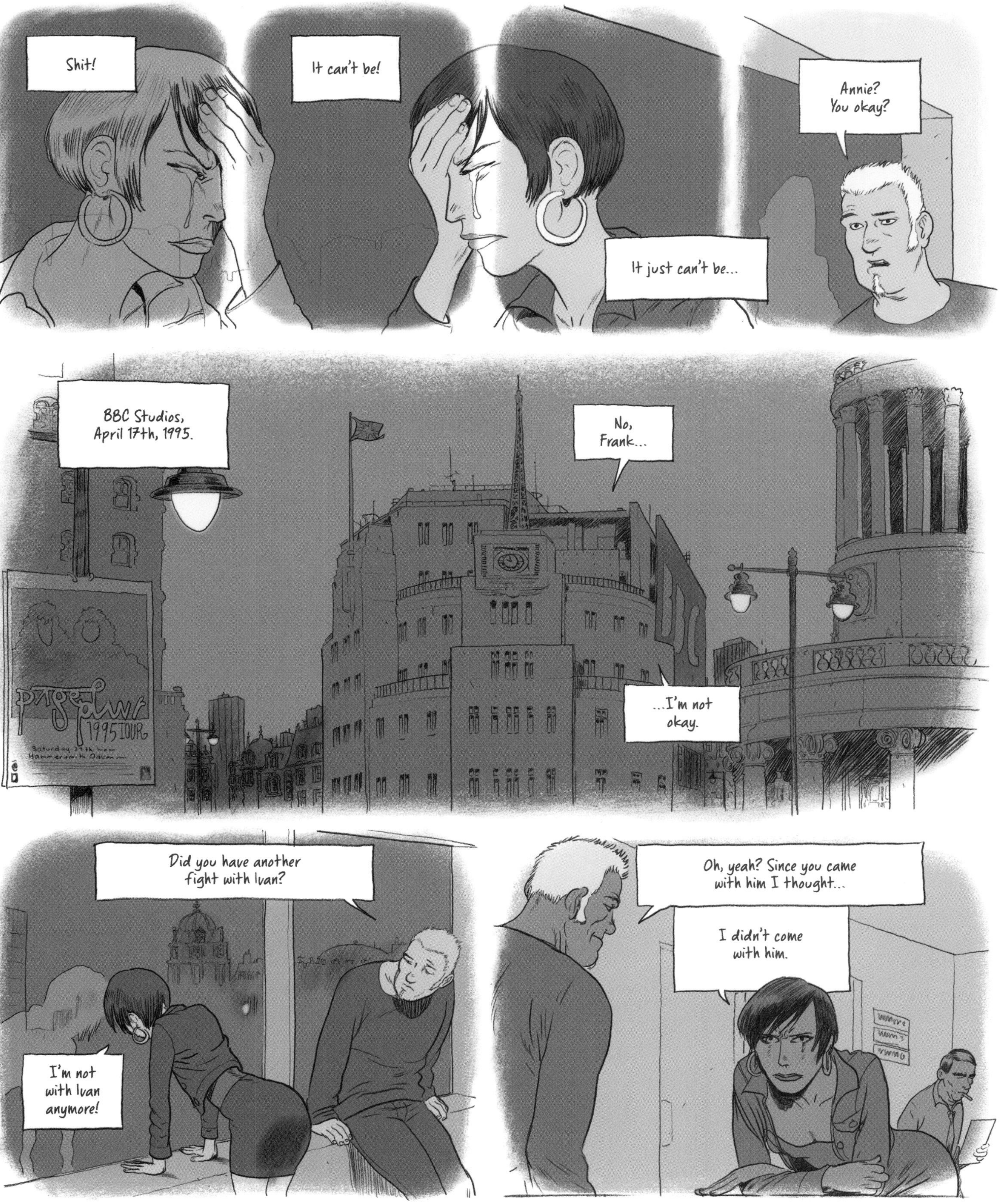
Shit!
It can't be!
It just can't be...
Annie? You okay?
BBC Studios, April 17th, 1995.
No, Frank...
...I'm not okay.
page plwr 1995 TOUR
Did you have another fight with Ivan?
I'm not with Ivan anymore!
Oh, yeah? Since you came with him I thought...
I didn't come with him.

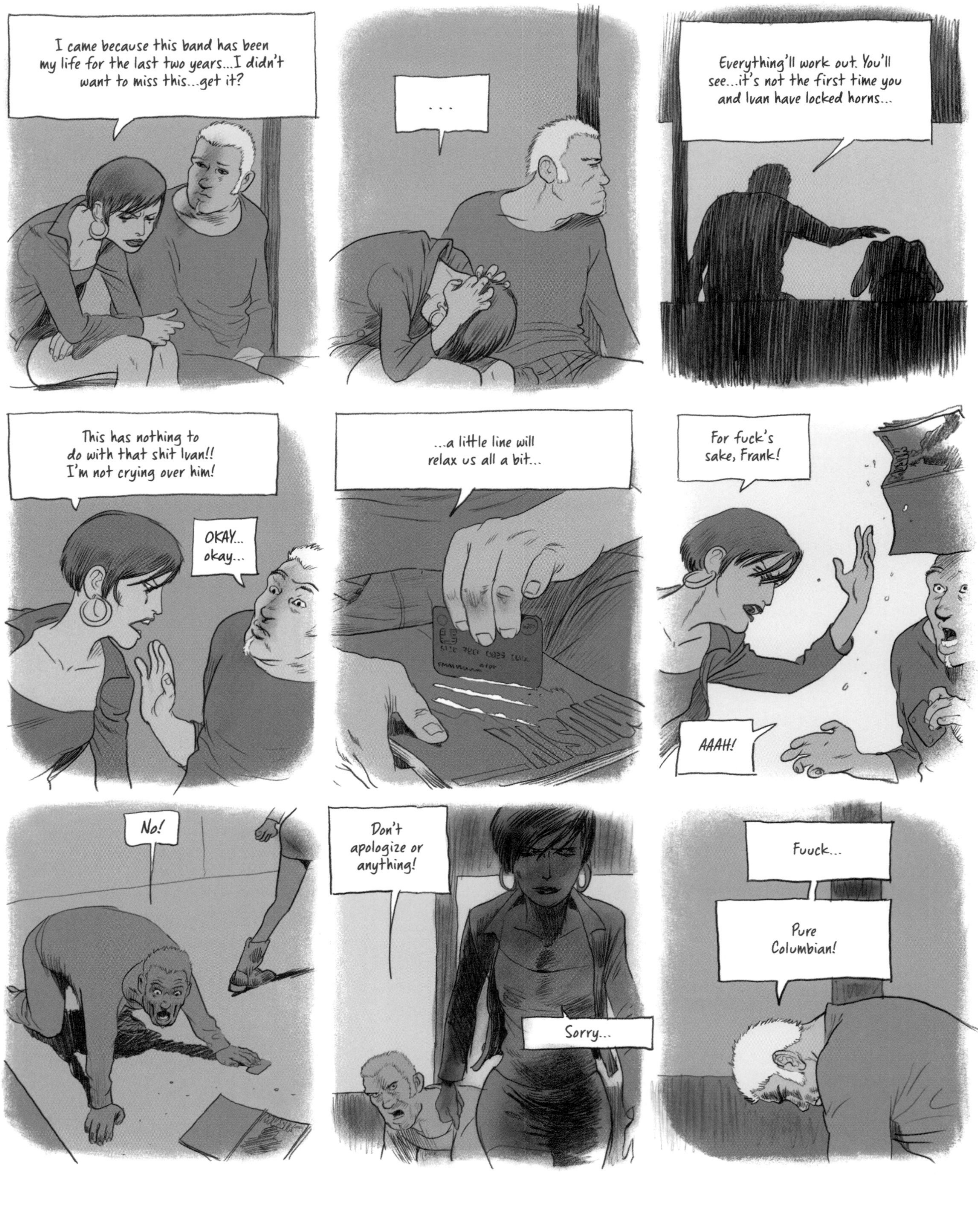
I came because this band has been my life for the last two years...I didn't want to miss this...get it?
. . .
Everything'll work out. You'll see...it's not the first time you and Ivan have locked horns...
This has nothing to do with that shit Ivan!! I'm not crying over him!
OKAY... okay...
...a little line will relax us all a bit...
For fuck's sake, Frank!
AAAH!
No!
Don't apologize or anything!
Sorry...
Fuuck...
Pure Columbian!

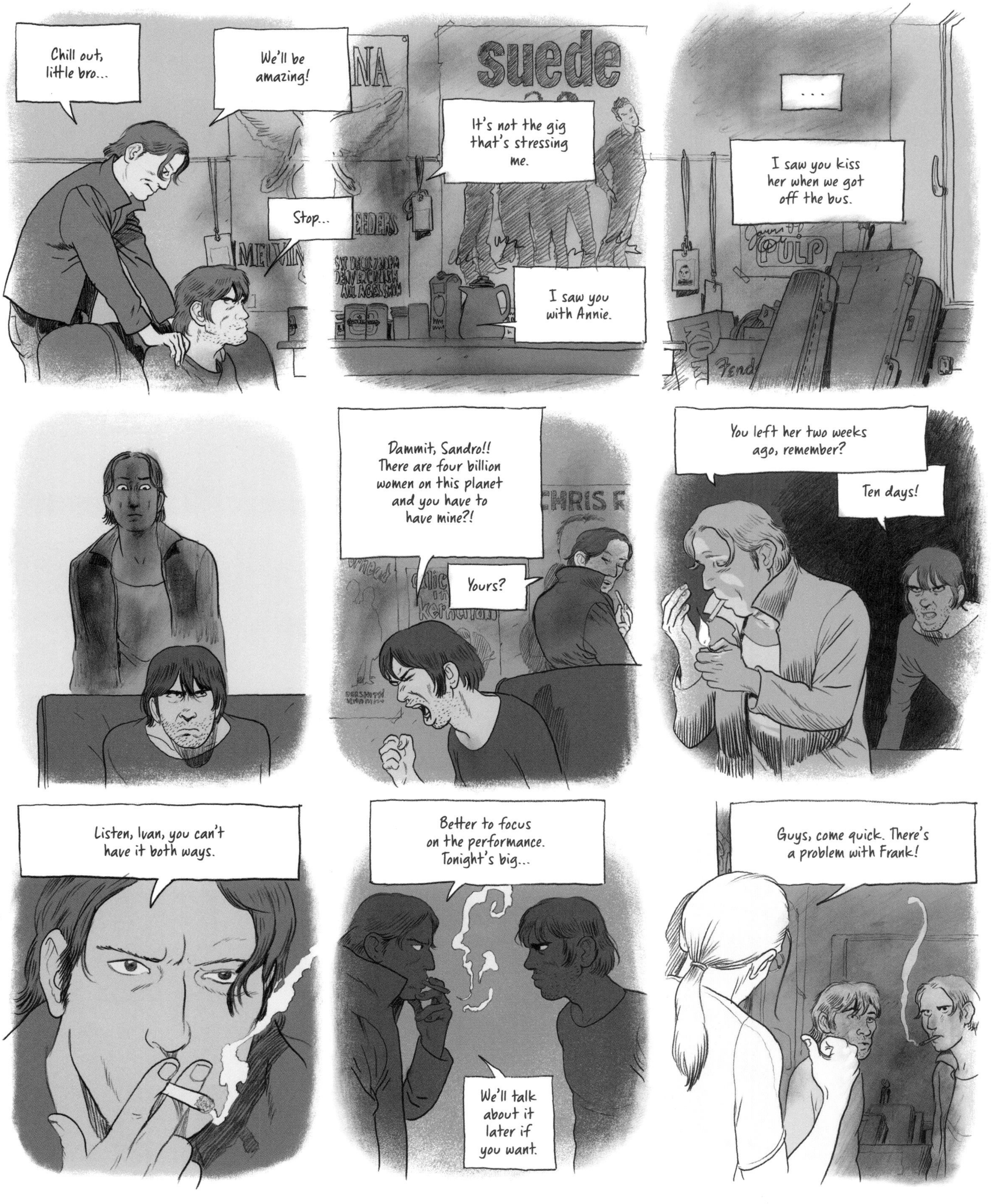
Chill out, little bro...
We'll be amazing!
It's not the gig that's stressing me.
Stop...
I saw you with Annie.
...
I saw you kiss her when we got off the bus.
Dammit, Sandro!! There are four billion women on this planet and you have to have mine?!
Yours?
You left her two weeks ago, remember?
Ten days!
Listen, Ivan, you can't have it both ways.
Better to focus on the performance. Tonight's big...
We'll talk about it later if you want.
Guys, come quick. There's a problem with Frank!

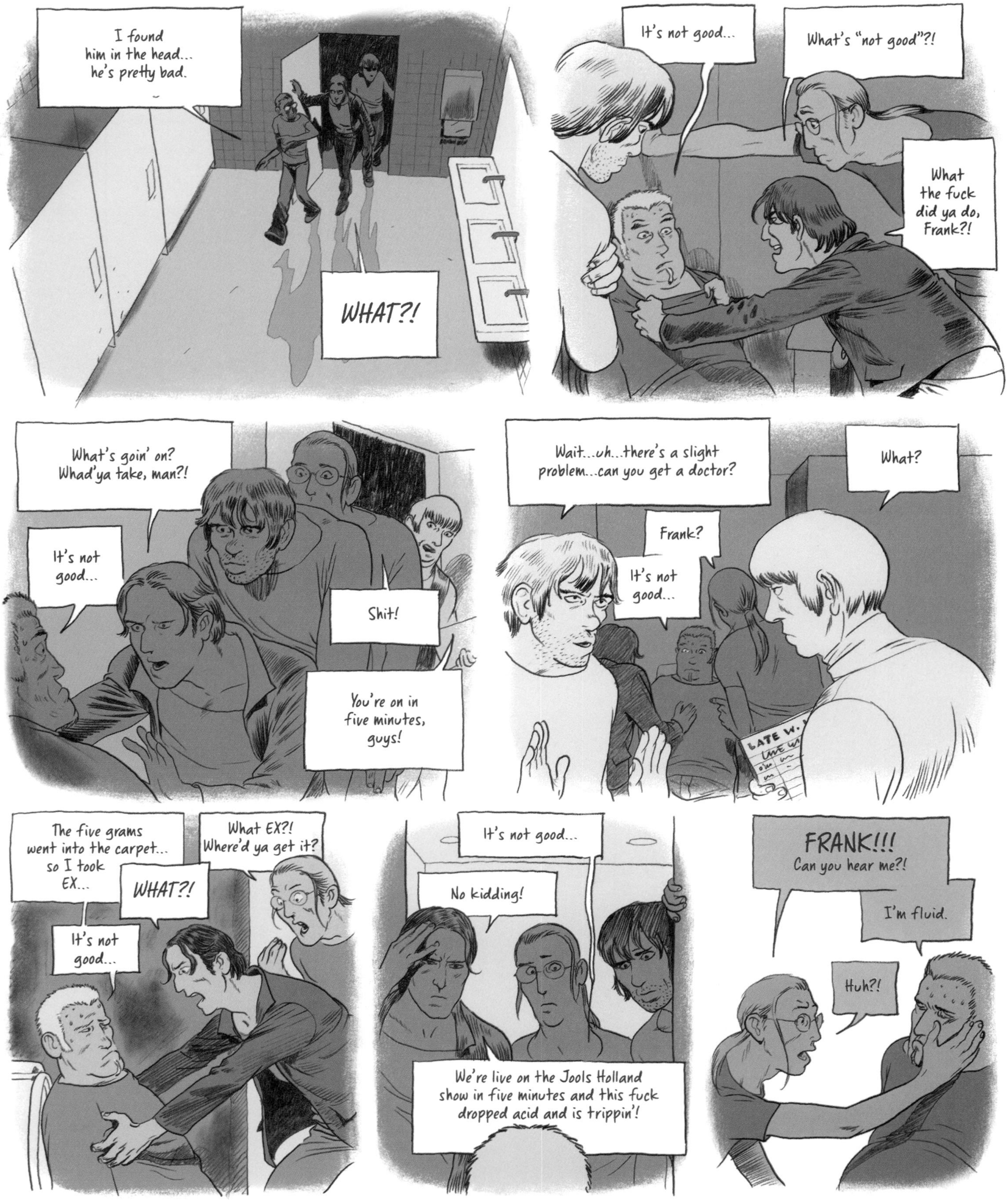

I found him in the head... he's pretty bad.
WHAT?!
It's not good...
What's "not good"?!
What the fuck did ya do, Frank?!
What's goin' on? Whad'ya take, man?!
It's not good...
Shit!
You're on in five minutes, guys!
Wait...uh...there's a slight problem...can you get a doctor?
What?
Frank?
It's not good...
The five grams went into the carpet... so I took EX...
What EX?! Where'd ya get it?
WHAT?!
It's not good...
It's not good...
No kidding!
We're live on the Jools Holland show in five minutes and this fuck dropped acid and is trippin'!
FRANK!!! Can you hear me?!
I'm fluid.
Huh?!

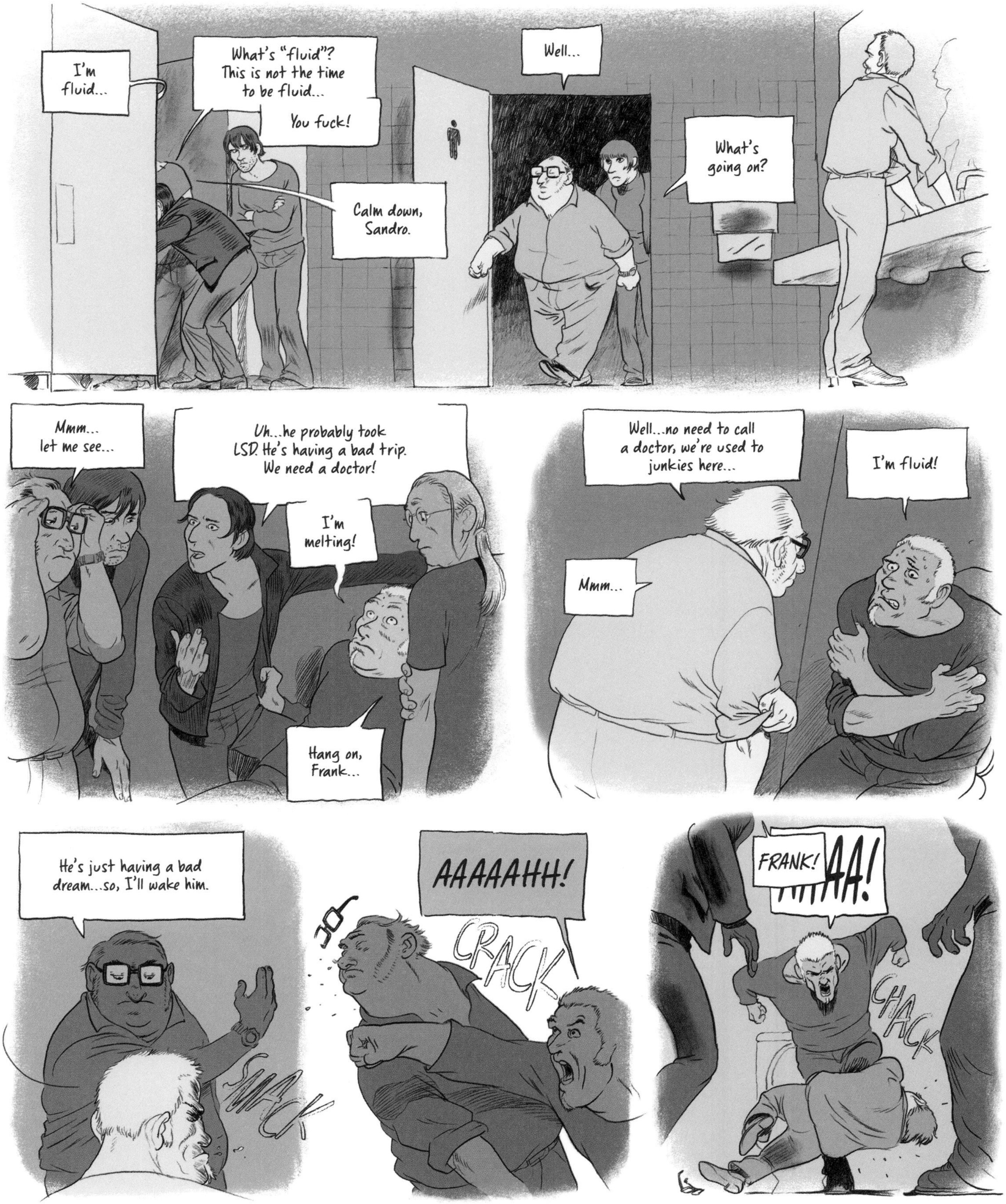

I'm fluid...
What's "fluid"? This is not the time to be fluid...
You fuck!
Calm down, Sandro.
Well...
What's going on?
Mmm... let me see...
Uh...he probably took LSD. He's having a bad trip. We need a doctor!
I'm melting!
Hang on, Frank...
Well...no need to call a doctor, we're used to junkies here...
Mmm...
I'm fluid!
He's just having a bad dream...so, I'll wake him.
SMACK
AAAAAHH!
CRACK
FRANK!
AA!
CHACK

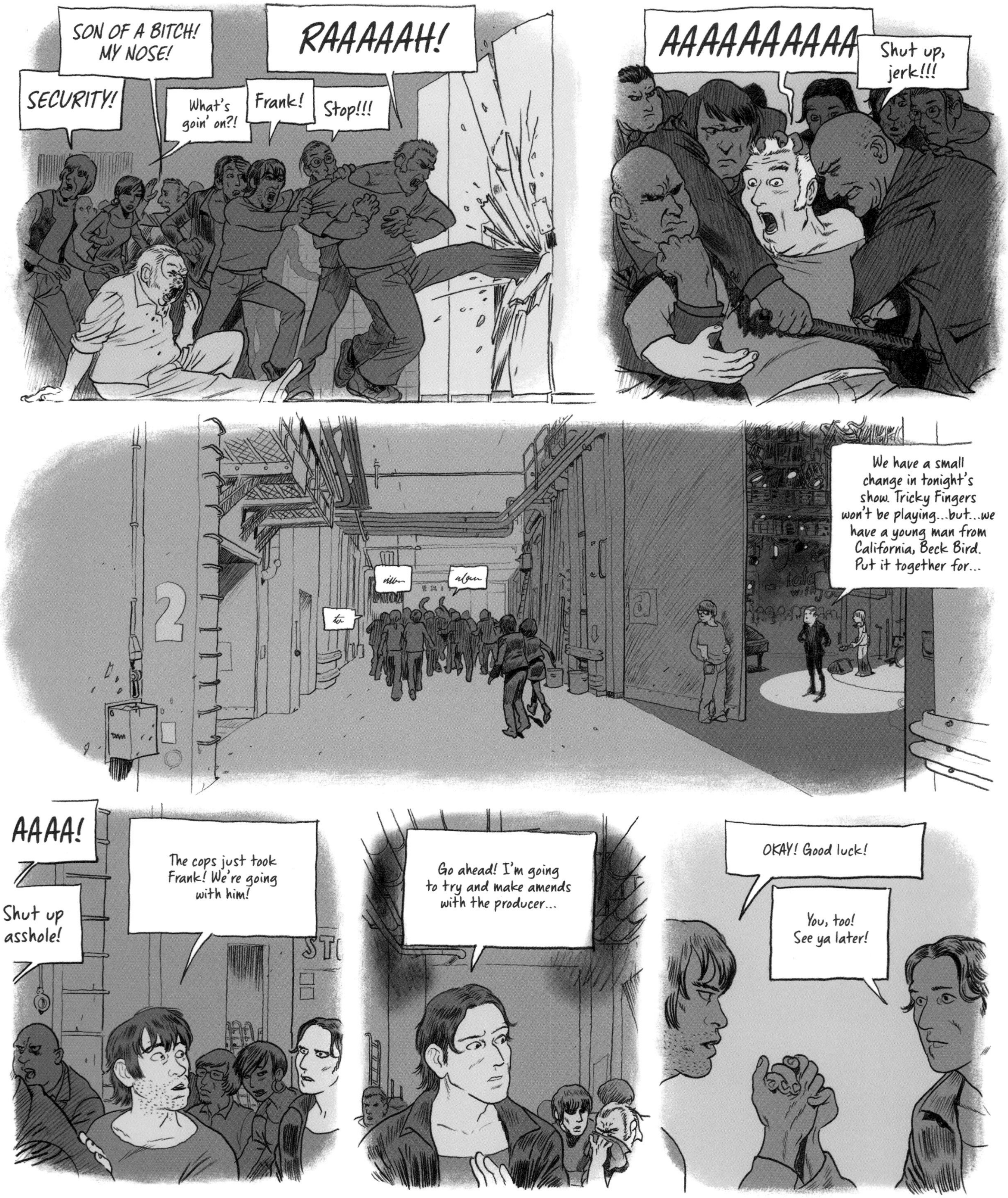
SON OF A BITCH! MY NOSE!
RAAAAAH!
SECURITY!
What's goin' on?!
Frank!
Stop!!!
AAAAAAAAAA
Shut up, jerk!!!
We have a small change in tonight's show. Tricky Fingers won't be playing...but...we have a young man from California, Beck Bird. Put it together for...
AAAA!
Shut up asshole!
The cops just took Frank! We're going with him!
Go ahead! I'm going to try and make amends with the producer...
OKAY! Good luck!
You, too! See ya later!

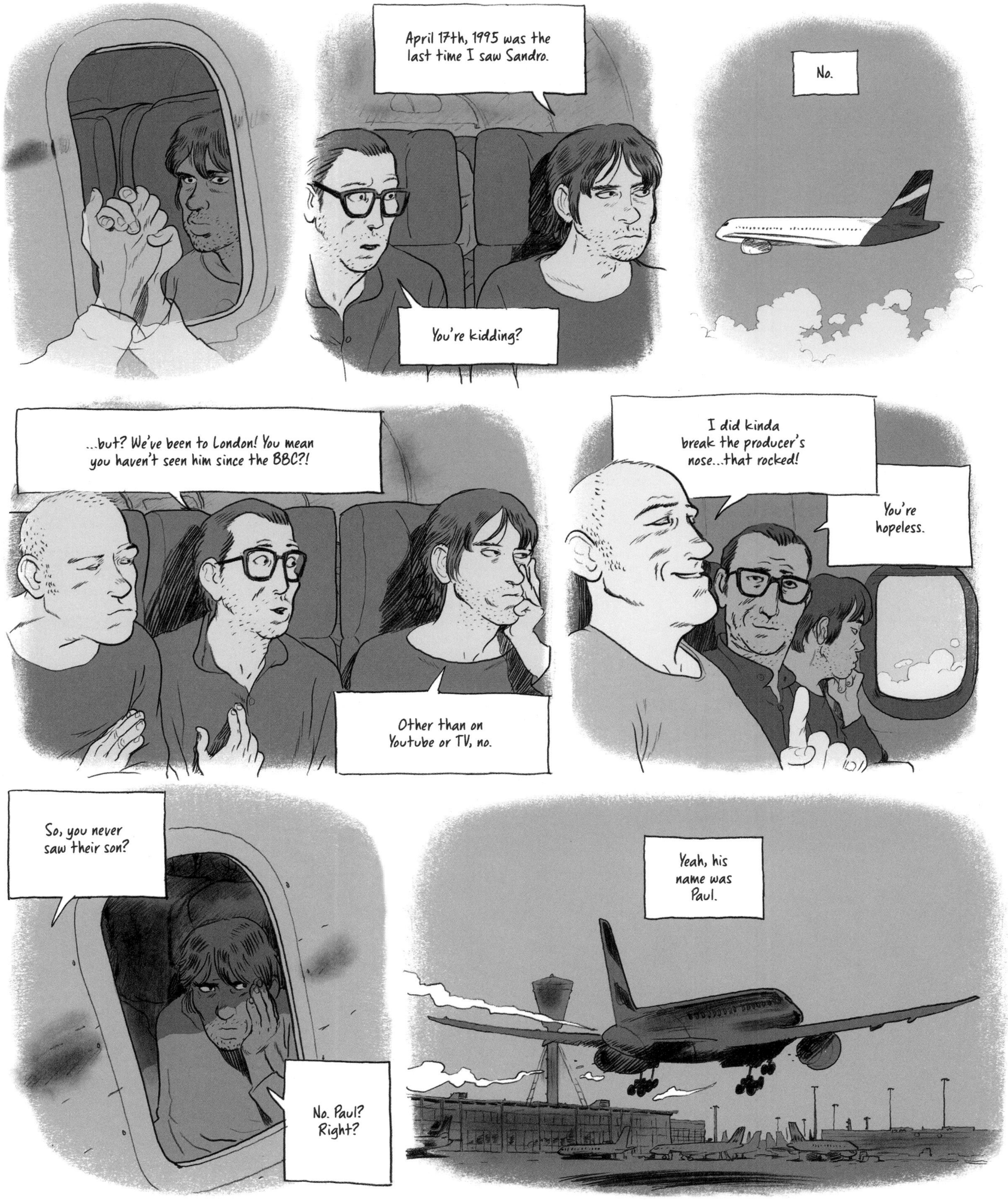

April 17th, 1995 was the last time I saw Sandro.
You're kidding?
No.
...but? We've been to London! You mean you haven't seen him since the BBC?!
Other than on Youtube or TV, no.
I did kinda break the producer's nose...that rocked!
You're hopeless.
So, you never saw their son?
No. Paul? Right?
Yeah, his name was Paul.

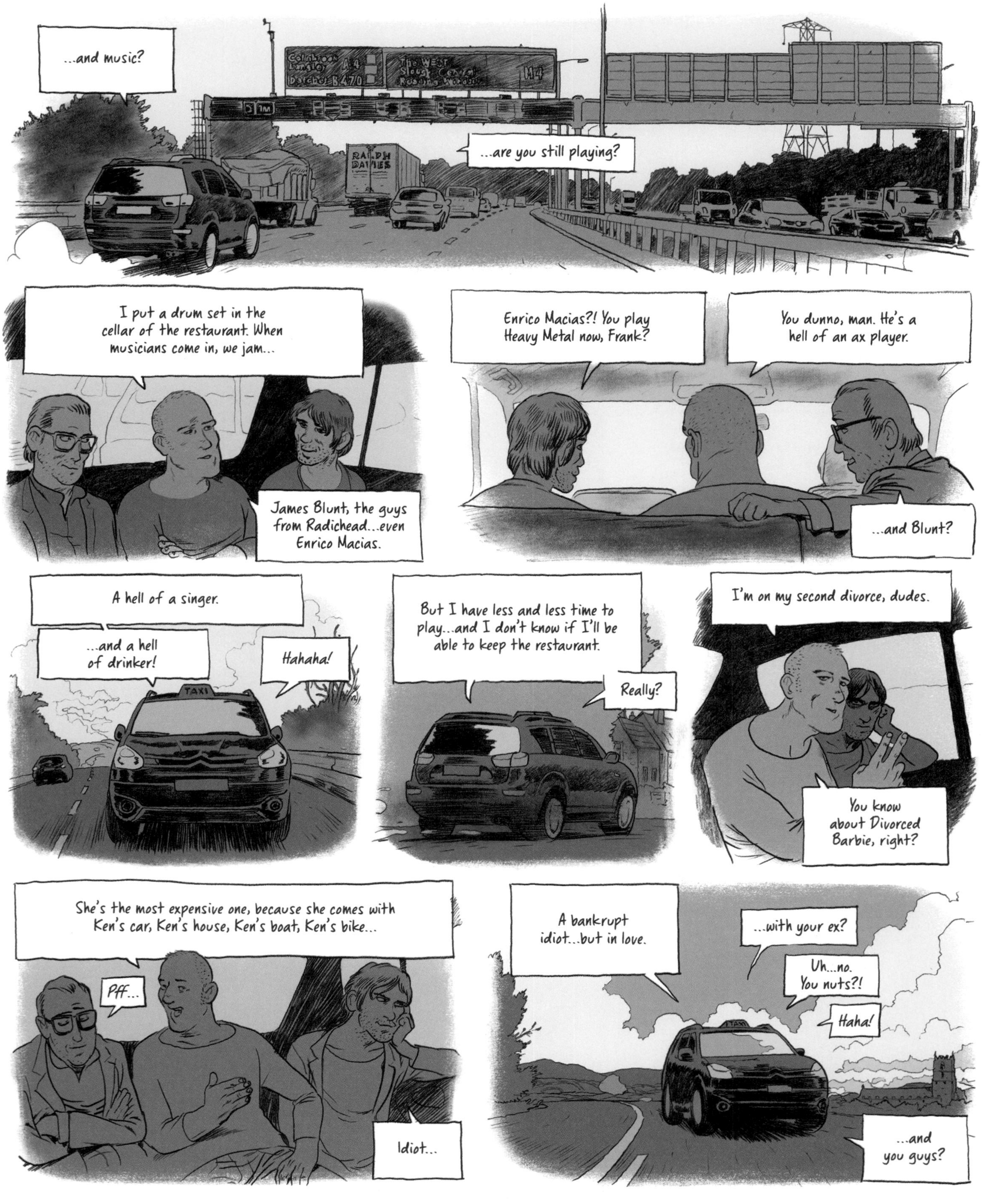
...and music?
...are you still playing?
I put a drum set in the cellar of the restaurant. When musicians come in, we jam...
James Blunt, the guys from Radichead...even Enrico Macias.
Enrico Macias?! You play Heavy Metal now, Frank?
You dunno, man. He's a hell of an ax player.
...and Blunt?
A hell of a singer.
...and a hell of drinker!
Hahaha!
But I have less and less time to play...and I don't know if I'll be able to keep the restaurant.
Really?
I'm on my second divorce, dudes.
You know about Divorced Barbie, right?
She's the most expensive one, because she comes with Ken's car, Ken's house, Ken's boat, Ken's bike...
Pff...
Idiot...
A bankrupt idiot...but in love.
...with your ex?
Uh...no. You nuts?!
Haha!
...and you guys?

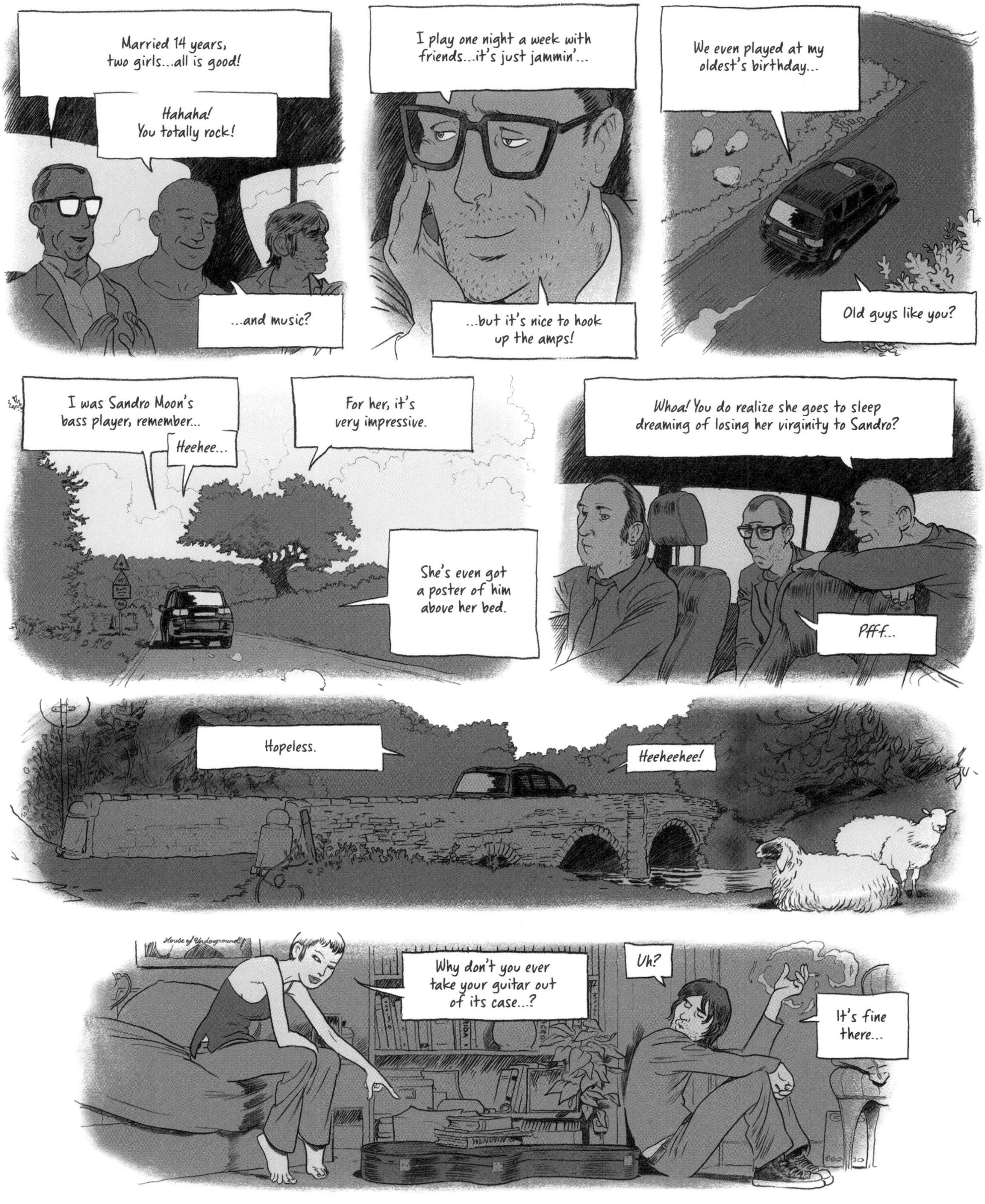
Married 14 years, two girls...all is good!
Hahaha! You totally rock!
...and music?
I play one night a week with friends...it's just jammin'...
...but it's nice to hook up the amps!
We even played at my oldest's birthday...
Old guys like you?
I was Sandro Moon's bass player, remember...
Heehee...
For her, it's very impressive.
She's even got a poster of him above her bed.
Whoa! You do realize she goes to sleep dreaming of losing her virginity to Sandro?
Pfff...
Hopeless.
Heeheehee!
Why don't you ever take your guitar out of its case...?
Uh?
It's fine there...

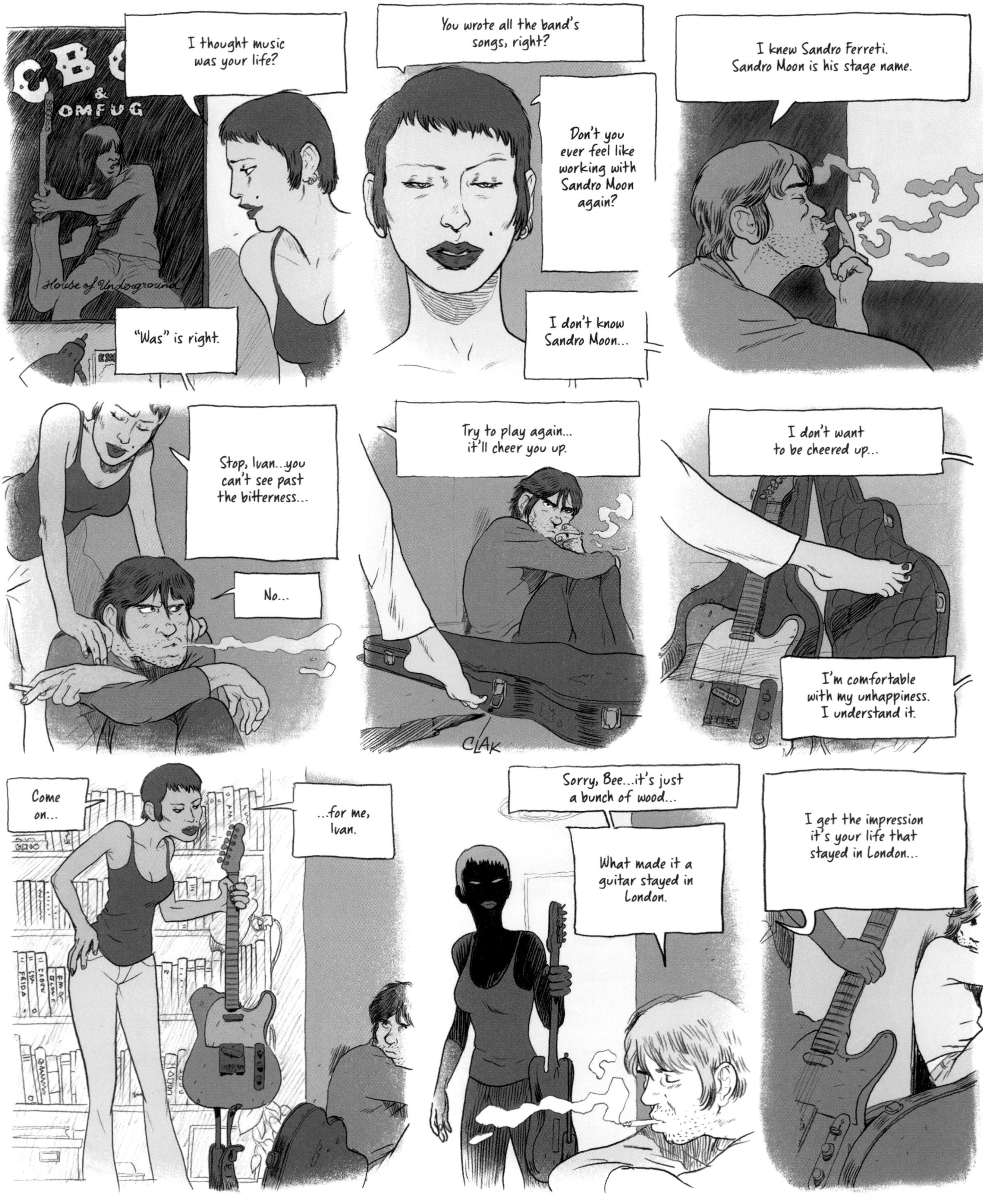
I thought music was your life?
"Was" is right.
CBGB & OMFUG
House of Underground
You wrote all the band's songs, right?
Don't you ever feel like working with Sandro Moon again?
I don't know Sandro Moon...
I knew Sandro Ferreti. Sandro Moon is his stage name.
Stop, Ivan...you can't see past the bitterness...
No...
Try to play again... it'll cheer you up.
CLAK
I don't want to be cheered up...
I'm comfortable with my unhappiness. I understand it.
Come on...
...for me, Ivan.
Sorry, Bee...it's just a bunch of wood...
What made it a guitar stayed in London.
I get the impression it's your life that stayed in London...

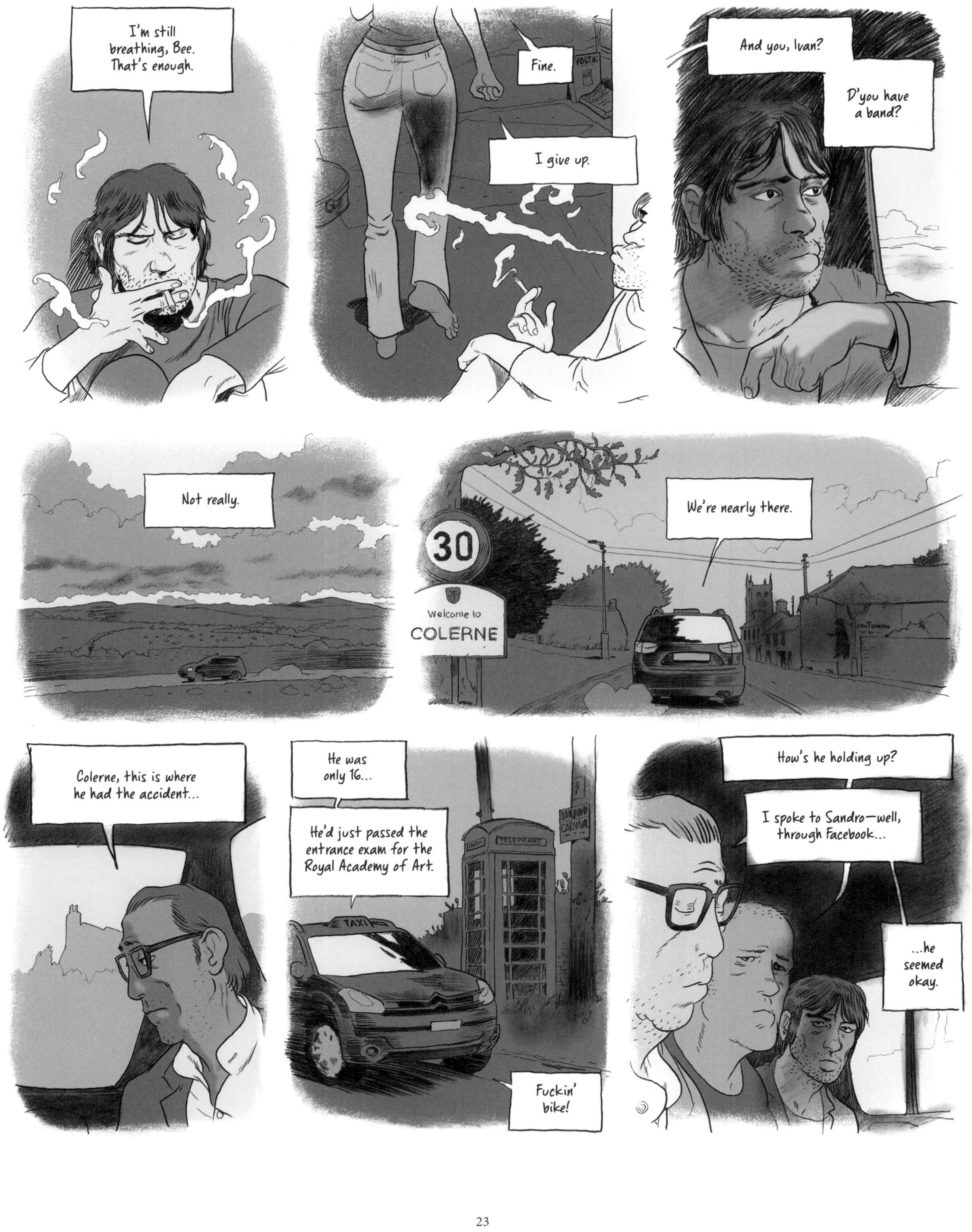
I'm still breathing, Bee. That's enough.
Fine.
I give up.
And you, Ivan?
D'you have a band?
Not really.
30
Welcome to COLERNE
We're nearly there.
Colerne, this is where he had the accident...
He was only 16...
He'd just passed the entrance exam for the Royal Academy of Art.
TAXI
TELEPHONE
Fuckin' bike!
How's he holding up?
I spoke to Sandro—well, through Facebook...
...he seemed okay.

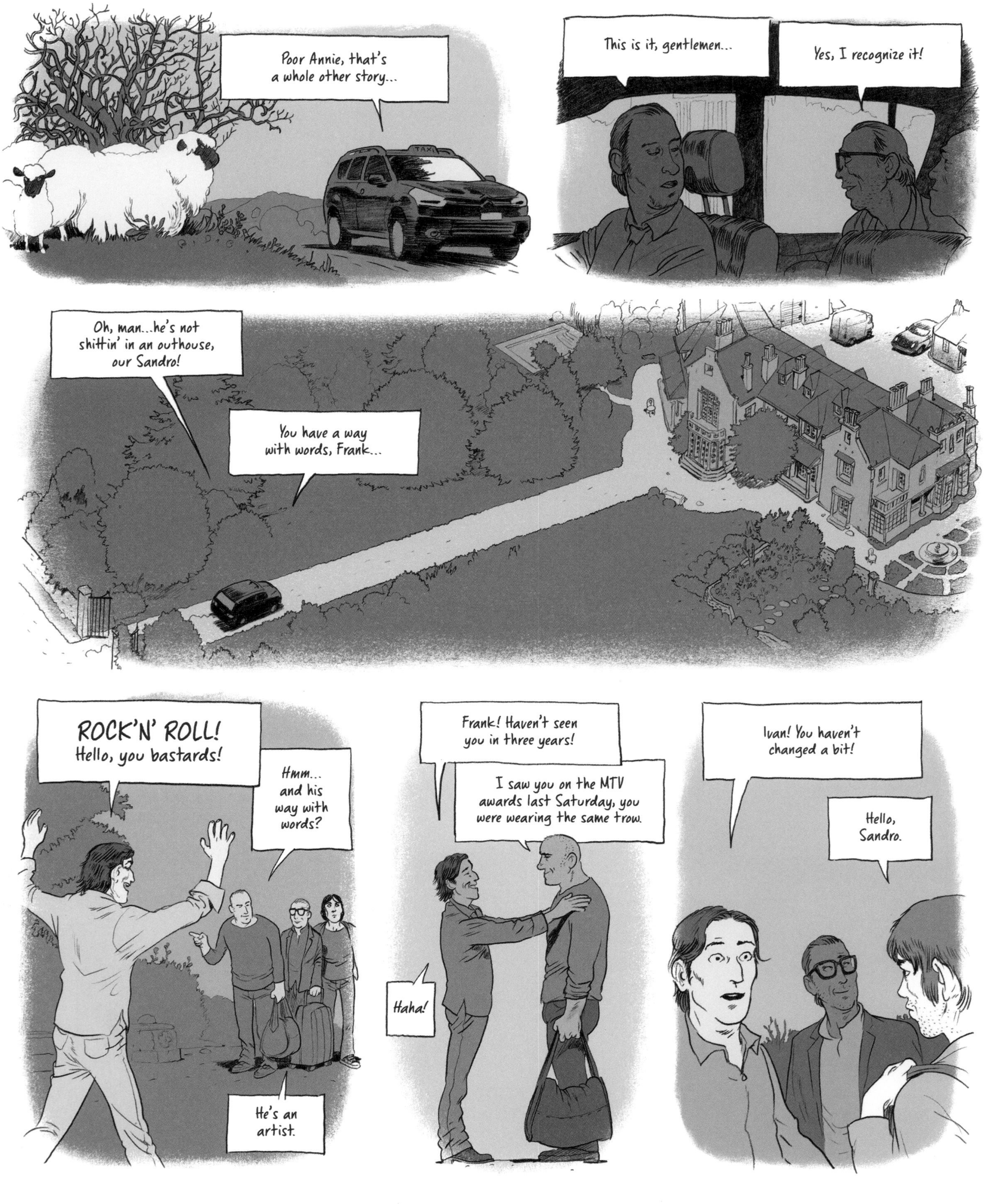

Poor Annie, that's a whole other story...
This is it, gentlemen...
Yes, I recognize it!
Oh, man...he's not shittin' in an outhouse, our Sandro!
You have a way with words, Frank...
ROCK'N' ROLL! Hello, you bastards!
Hmm... and his way with words?
He's an artist.
Frank! Haven't seen you in three years!
I saw you on the MTV awards last Saturday, you were wearing the same trow.
Haha!
Ivan! You haven't changed a bit!
Hello, Sandro.

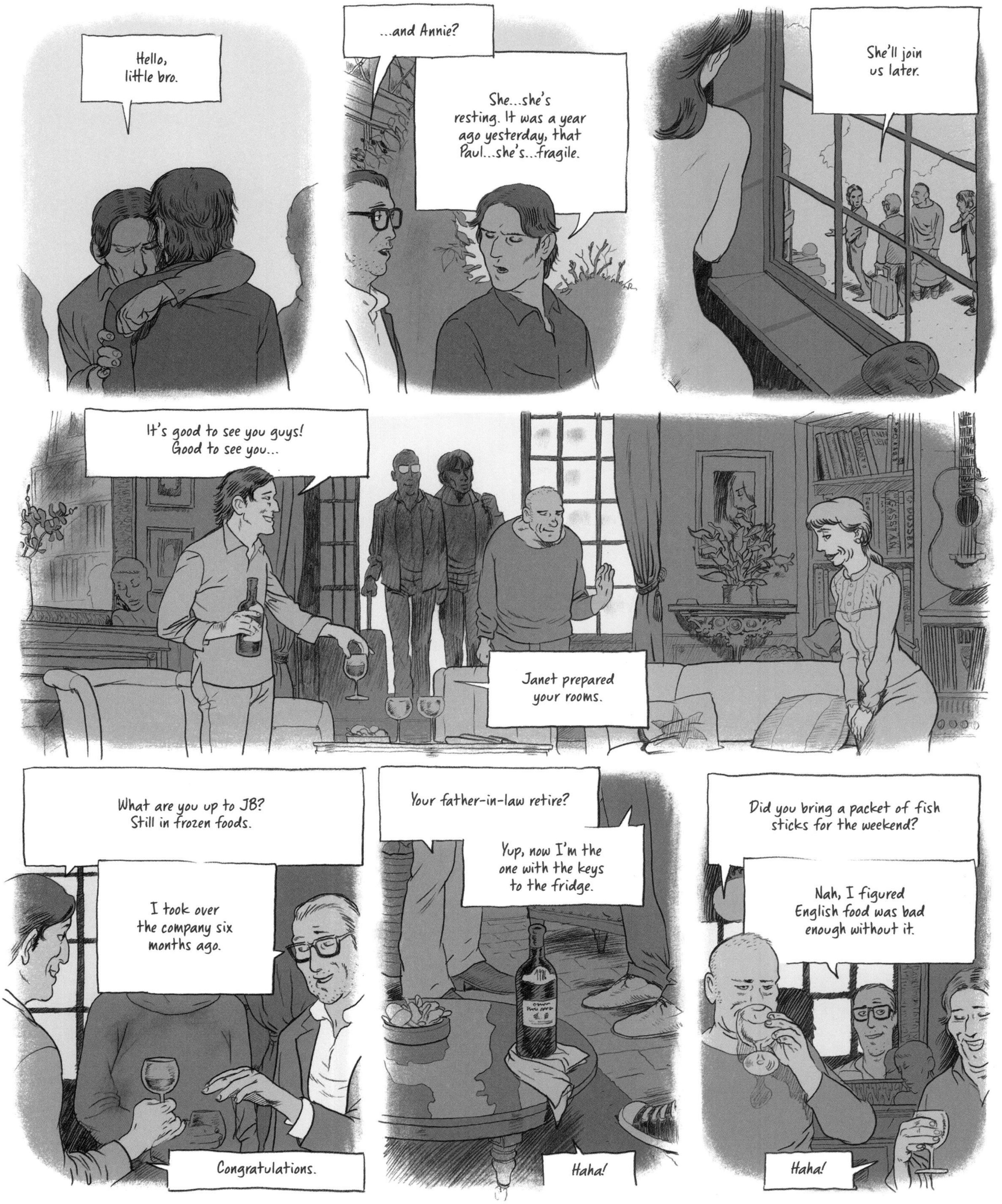
Hello, little bro.
...and Annie?
She...she's resting. It was a year ago yesterday, that Paul...she's...fragile.
She'll join us later.
It's good to see you guys! Good to see you...
Janet prepared your rooms.
What are you up to JB? Still in frozen foods.
I took over the company six months ago.
Congratulations.
Your father-in-law retire?
Yup, now I'm the one with the keys to the fridge.
Haha!
Did you bring a packet of fish sticks for the weekend?
Nah, I figured English food was bad enough without it.
Haha!

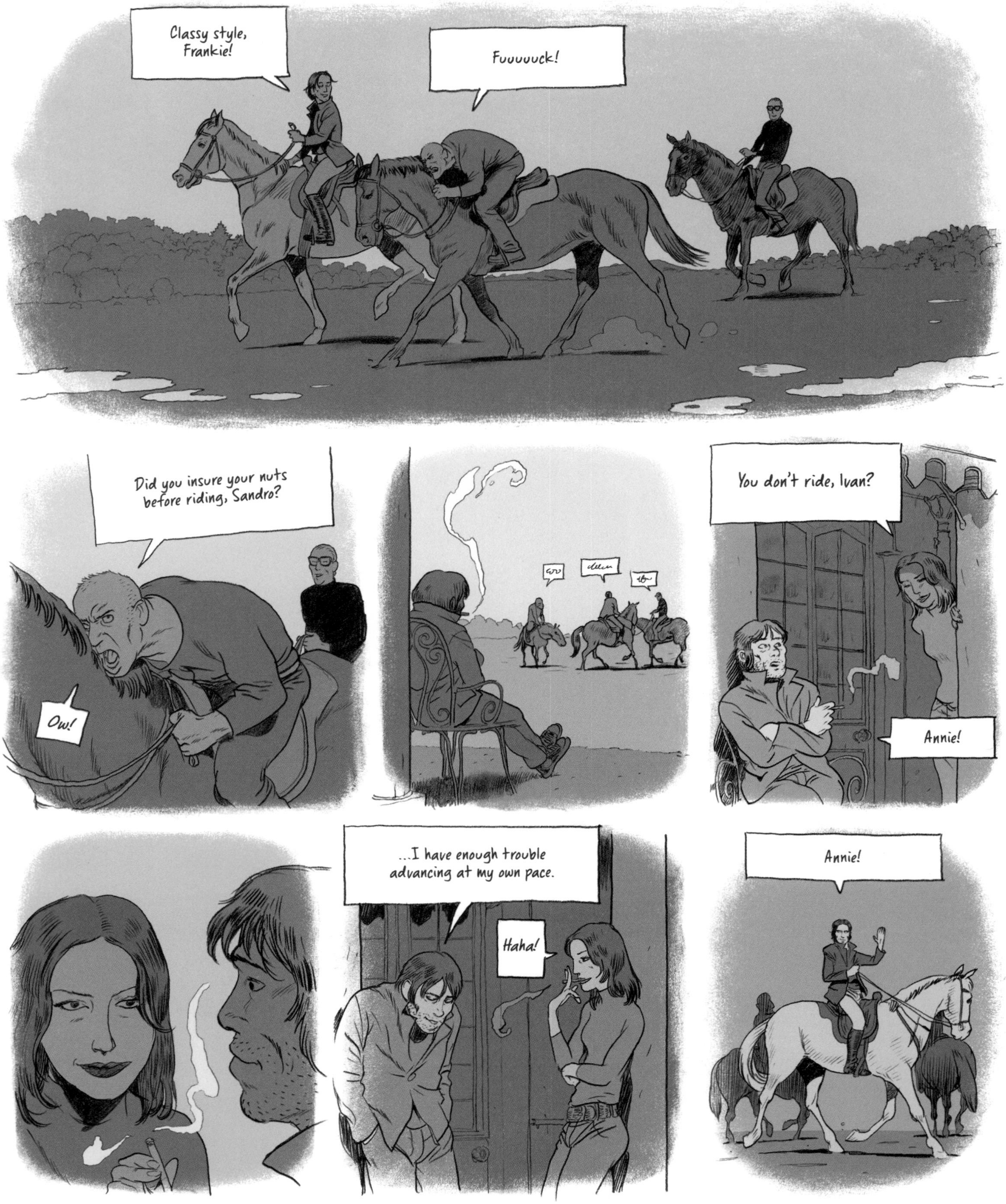
Classy style, Frankie!
Fuuuuuck!
Did you insure your nuts before riding, Sandro?
Ow!
You don't ride, Ivan?
Annie!
...I have enough trouble advancing at my own pace.
Haha!
Annie!

Sometimes I wish he'd fall off...

It's good to see you, Ivan...

You, too...

Wait til you taste Janet's Stilton sausages... they're amazing!

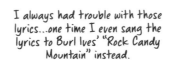

Mmm...

I'd rather eat horse.

Do you guys remember the time Sandro couldn't remember the lyrics to "Silent Girl" and he sung the ones from "Blue Suede Shoes" instead?

Yeah!

I always had trouble with those lyrics...one time I even sang the lyrics to Burl Ives' "Rock Candy Mountain" instead.

Haha!

No?

"On a summer's day...in the month of May..."...but the sound system was so bad you guys didn't even notice!

Haha!

And the sausage?

Not bad.

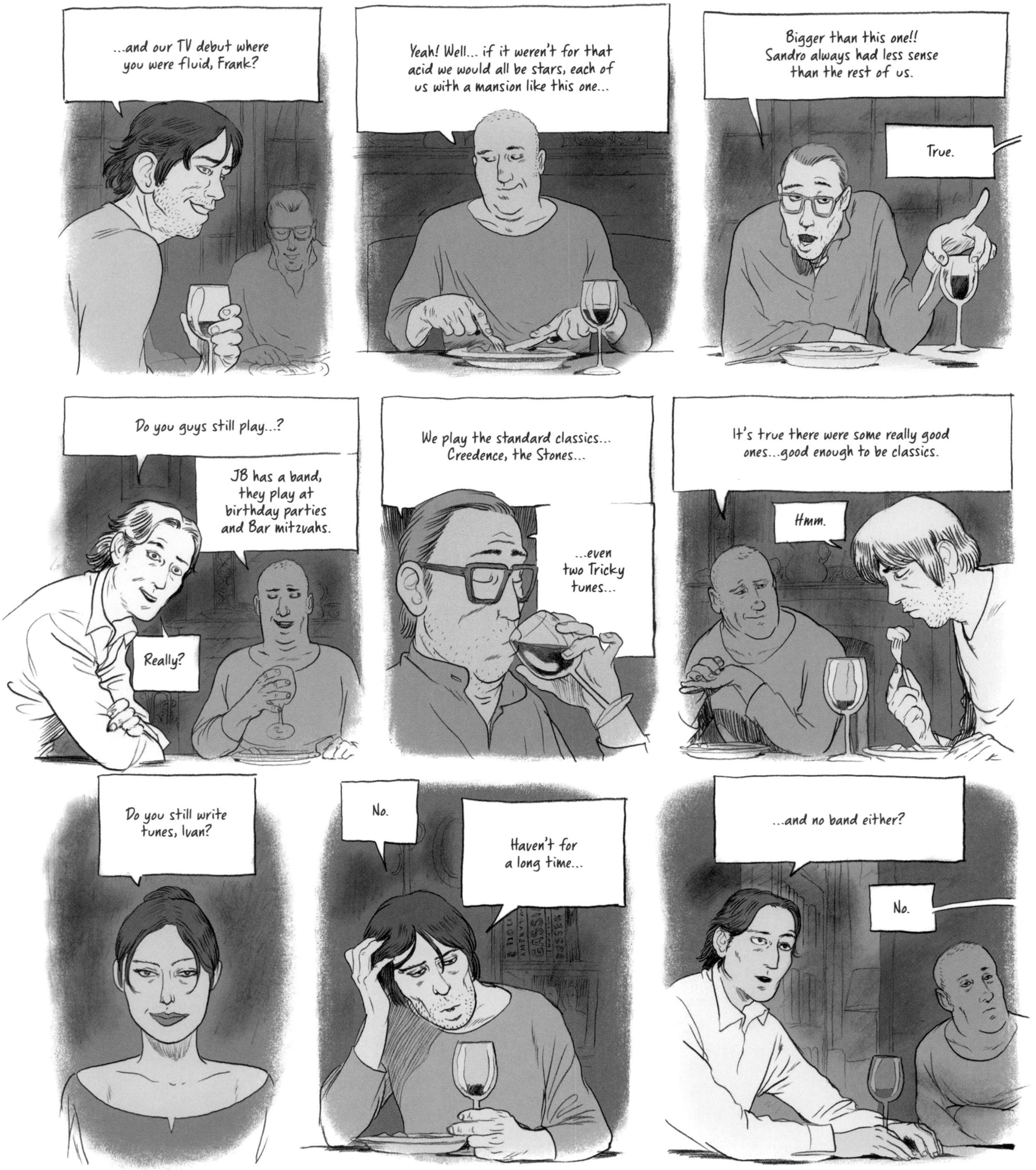
...and our TV debut where you were fluid, Frank?
Yeah! Well... if it weren't for that acid we would all be stars, each of us with a mansion like this one...
Bigger than this one!! Sandro always had less sense than the rest of us.
True.
Do you guys still play...?
JB has a band, they play at birthday parties and Bar mitzvahs.
Really?
We play the standard classics... Creedence, the Stones...
...even two Tricky tunes...
It's true there were some really good ones...good enough to be classics.
Hmm.
Do you still write tunes, Ivan?
No.
Haven't for a long time...
...and no band either?
No.

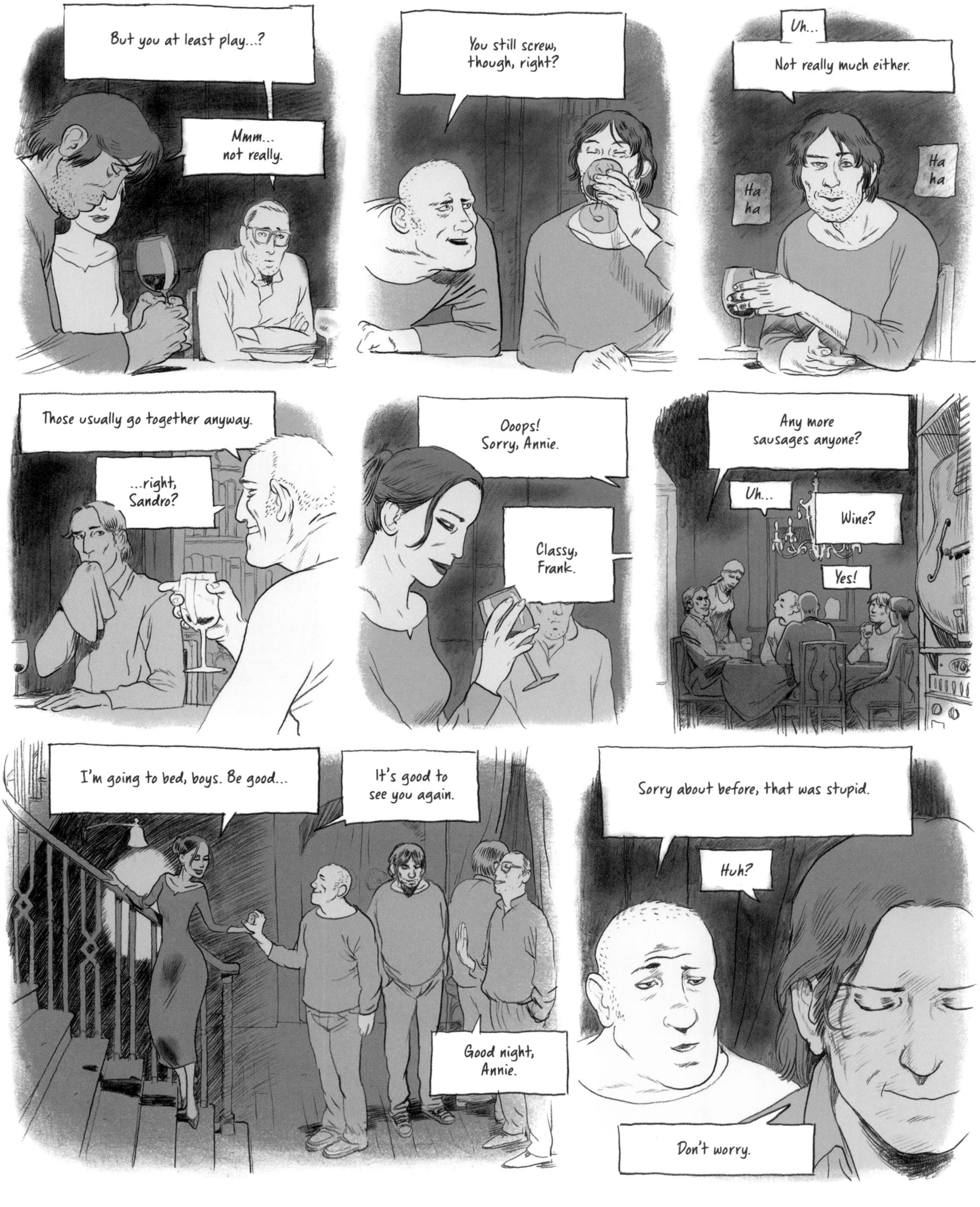
But you at least play...?
Mmm... not really.
You still screw, though, right?
Uh...
Not really much either.
Ha ha
Ha ha
Those usually go together anyway.
...right, Sandro?
Ooops! Sorry, Annie.
Classy, Frank.
Any more sausages anyone?
Uh...
Wine?
Yes!
I'm going to bed, boys. Be good...
It's good to see you again.
Good night, Annie.
Sorry about before, that was stupid.
Huh?
Don't worry.

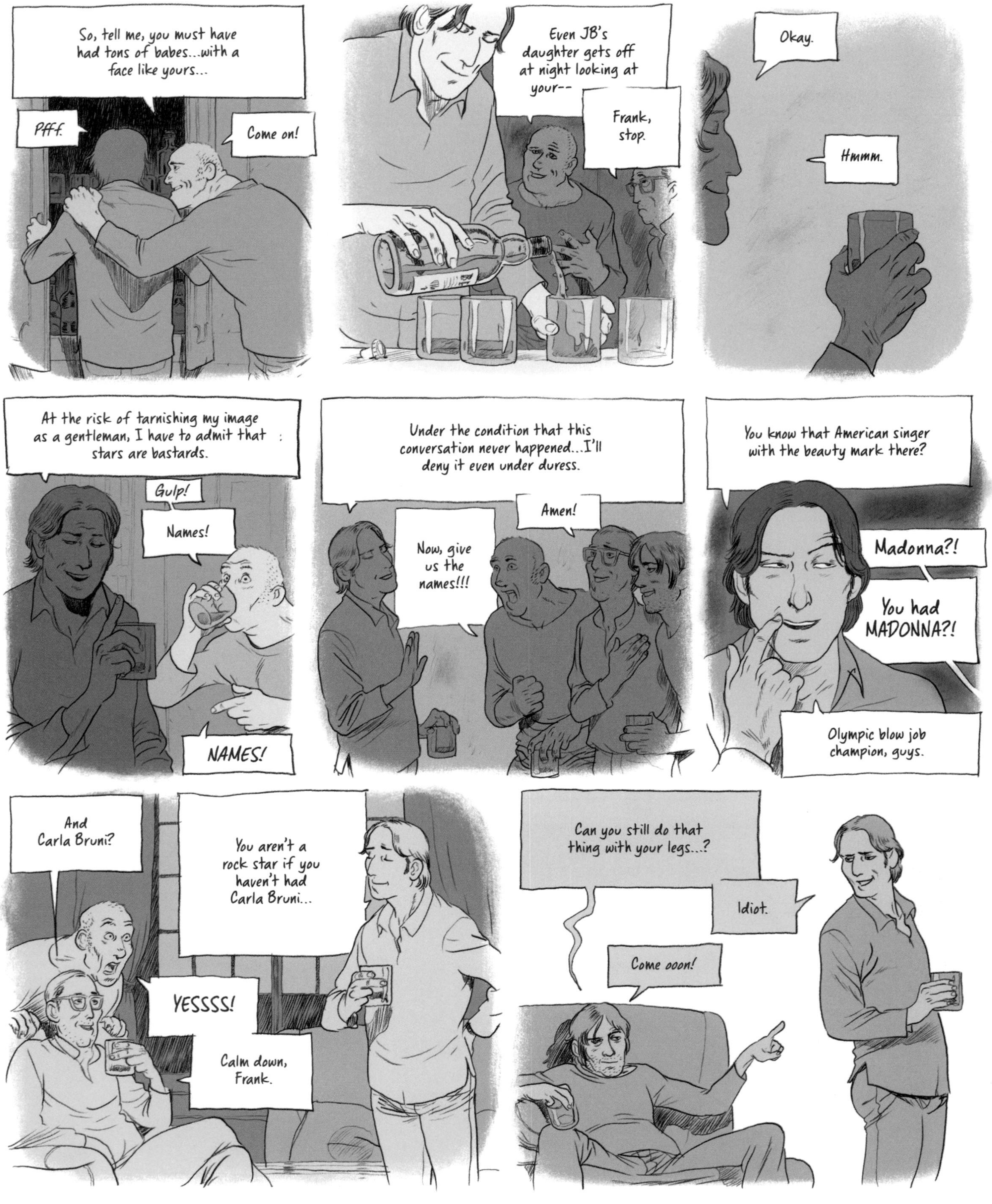

So, tell me, you must have had tons of babes...with a face like yours...
Pfff.
Come on!
Even JB's daughter gets off at night looking at your--
Frank, stop.
Okay.
Hmmm.
At the risk of tarnishing my image as a gentleman, I have to admit that stars are bastards.
Gulp!
Names!
NAMES!
Under the condition that this conversation never happened...I'll deny it even under duress.
Amen!
Now, give us the names!!!
You know that American singer with the beauty mark there?
Madonna?!
You had MADONNA?!
Olympic blow job champion, guys.
And Carla Bruni?
You aren't a rock star if you haven't had Carla Bruni...
YESSSS!
Calm down, Frank.
Can you still do that thing with your legs...?
Idiot.
Come ooon!

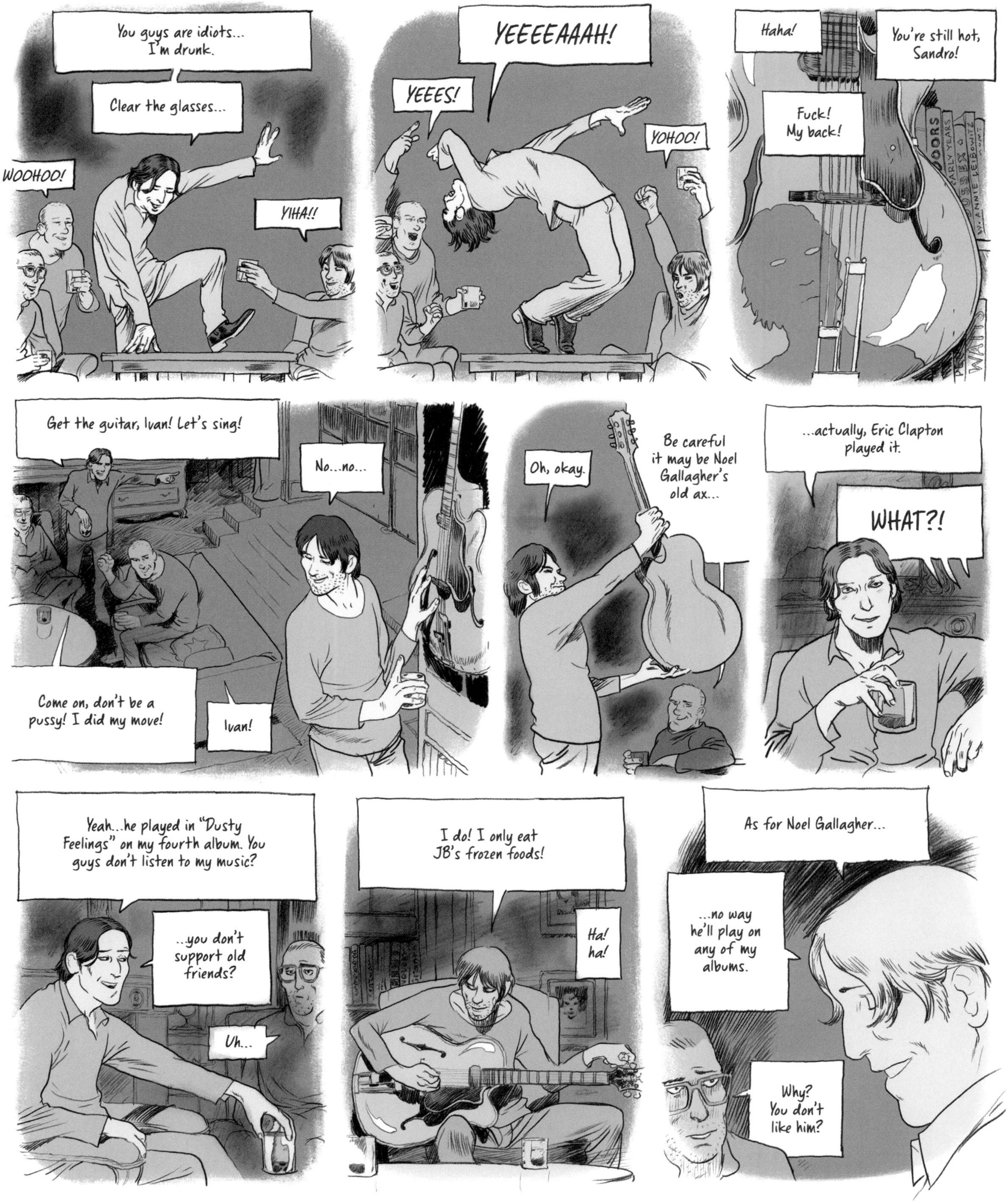
You guys are idiots... I'm drunk.
Clear the glasses...
WOOHOO!
YIHA!!
YEEEEAAAH!
YEEES!
YOHOO!
Haha!
You're still hot, Sandro!
Fuck! My back!
Get the guitar, Ivan! Let's sing!
No...no...
Come on, don't be a pussy! I did my move!
Ivan!
Oh, okay.
Be careful it may be Noel Gallagher's old ax...
...actually, Eric Clapton played it.
WHAT?!
Yeah...he played in "Dusty Feelings" on my fourth album. You guys don't listen to my music?
...you don't support old friends?
Uh...
I do! I only eat JB's frozen foods!
Ha! ha!
As for Noel Gallagher...
...no way he'll play on any of my albums.
Why? You don't like him?

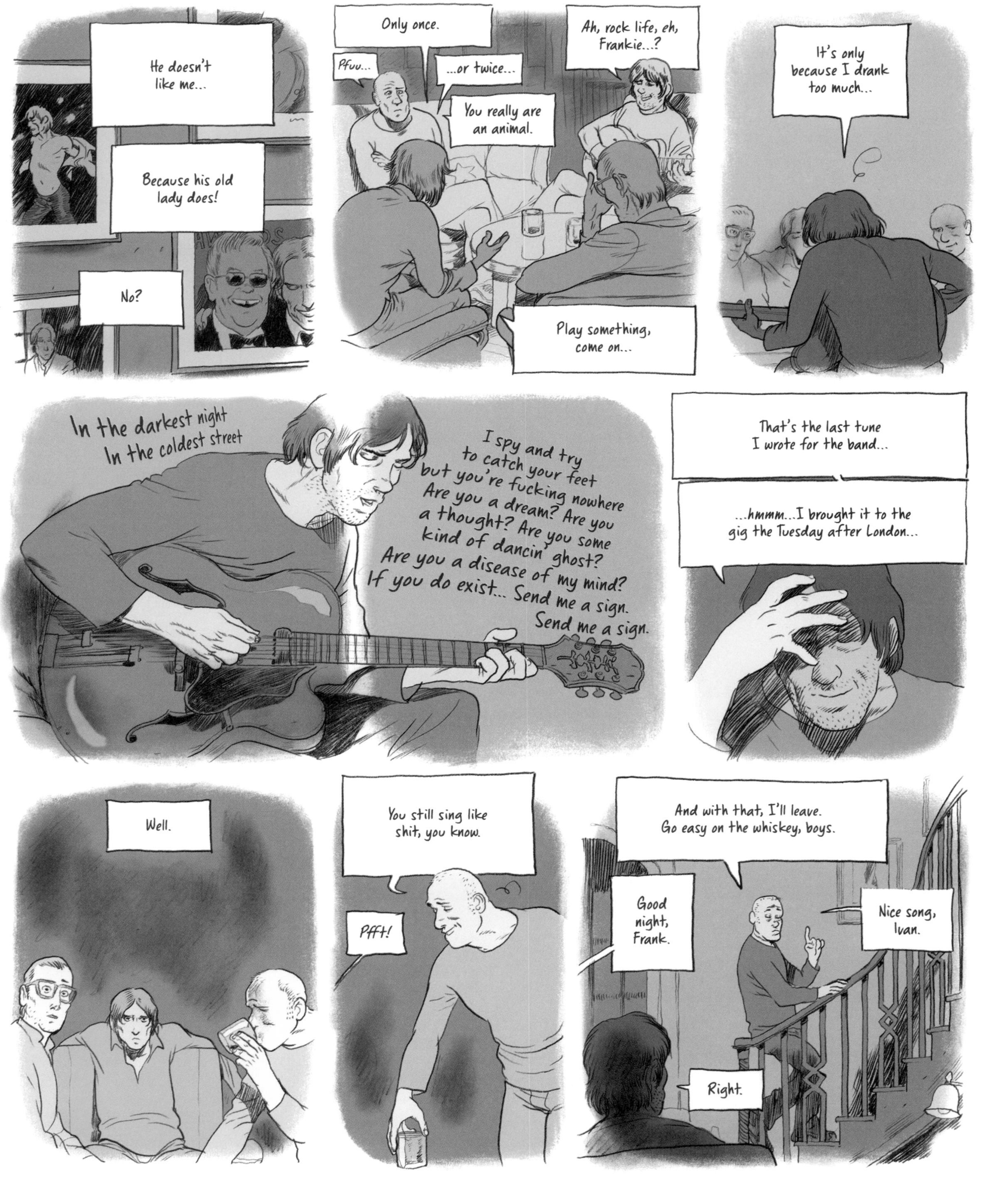

He doesn't like me...
Because his old lady does!
No?
Only once.
Pfuu...
...or twice...
You really are an animal.
Ah, rock life, eh, Frankie...?
Play something, come on...
It's only because I drank too much...
In the darkest night
In the coldest street
I spy and try to catch your feet but you're fucking nowhere Are you a dream? Are you a thought? Are you some kind of dancin' ghost? Are you a disease of my mind? If you do exist... Send me a sign. Send me a sign.
That's the last tune I wrote for the band...
...hmmm...I brought it to the gig the Tuesday after London...
Well.
You still sing like shit, you know.
Pfft!
And with that, I'll leave. Go easy on the whiskey, boys.
Good night, Frank.
Nice song, Ivan.
Right.

Sandro?

Mmm.

You and Annie...you didn't want more kids?

Sorry, it's none of my business.

No, no, it's okay.

...actually, I can't have any.

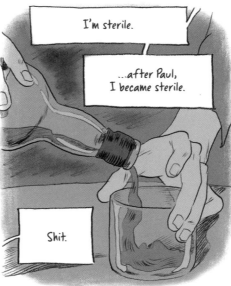

I'm sterile.

...after Paul, I became sterile.

Shit.

I'm also sterile.

AND YOU SING LIKE SHIT!

HA! HA! HA!

Shut up, Frank!

Jerk!

Go to bed!

I'm going, too. I'm exhausted.

Ivan...

Mm?

...amazing tune...

Yeah, thanks.

It came a bit late...

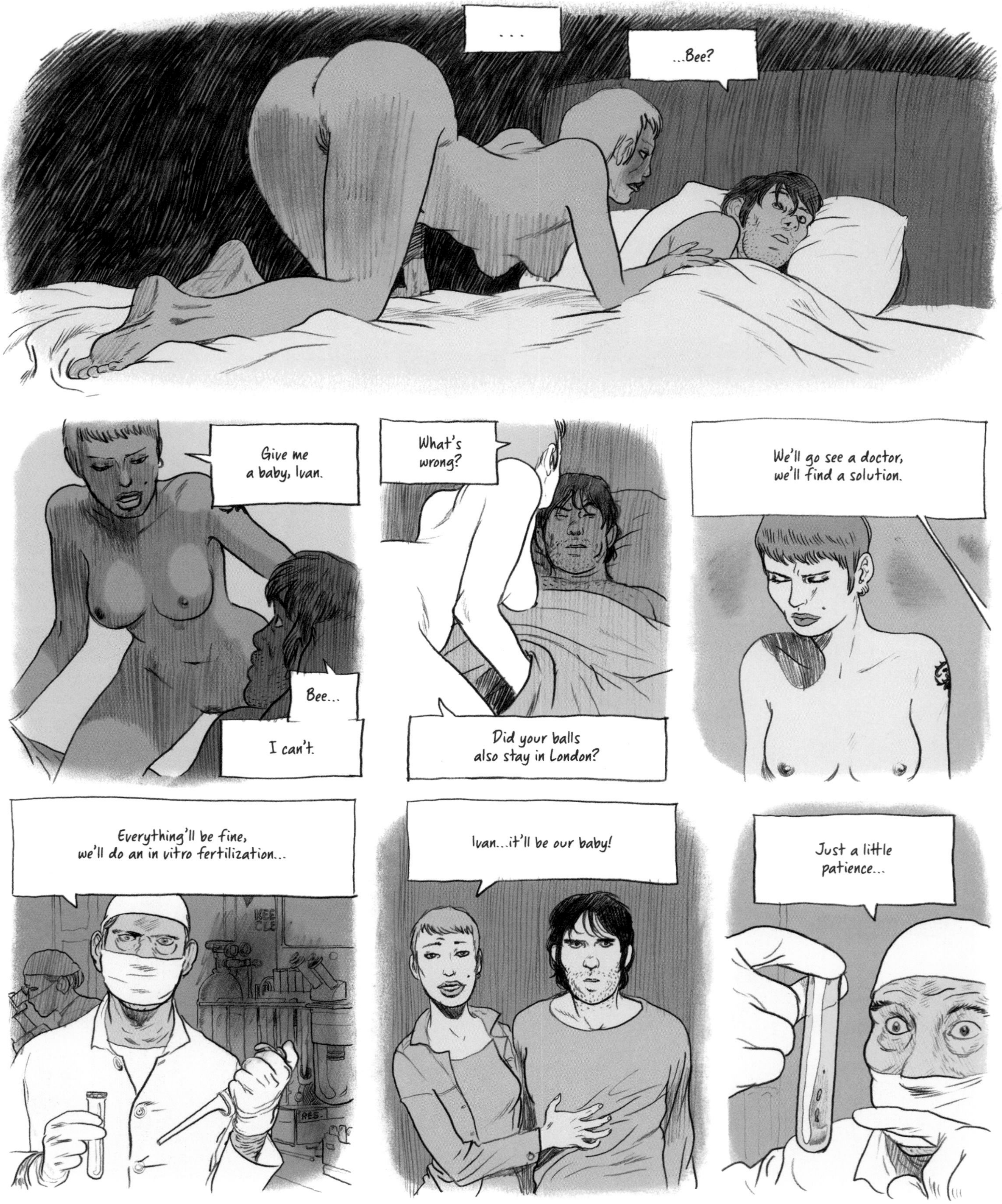
. . .
...Bee?
Give me a baby, Ivan.
Bee...
I can't.
What's wrong?
Did your balls also stay in London?
We'll go see a doctor, we'll find a solution.
Everything'll be fine, we'll do an in vitro fertilization...
Ivan...it'll be our baby!
Just a little patience...

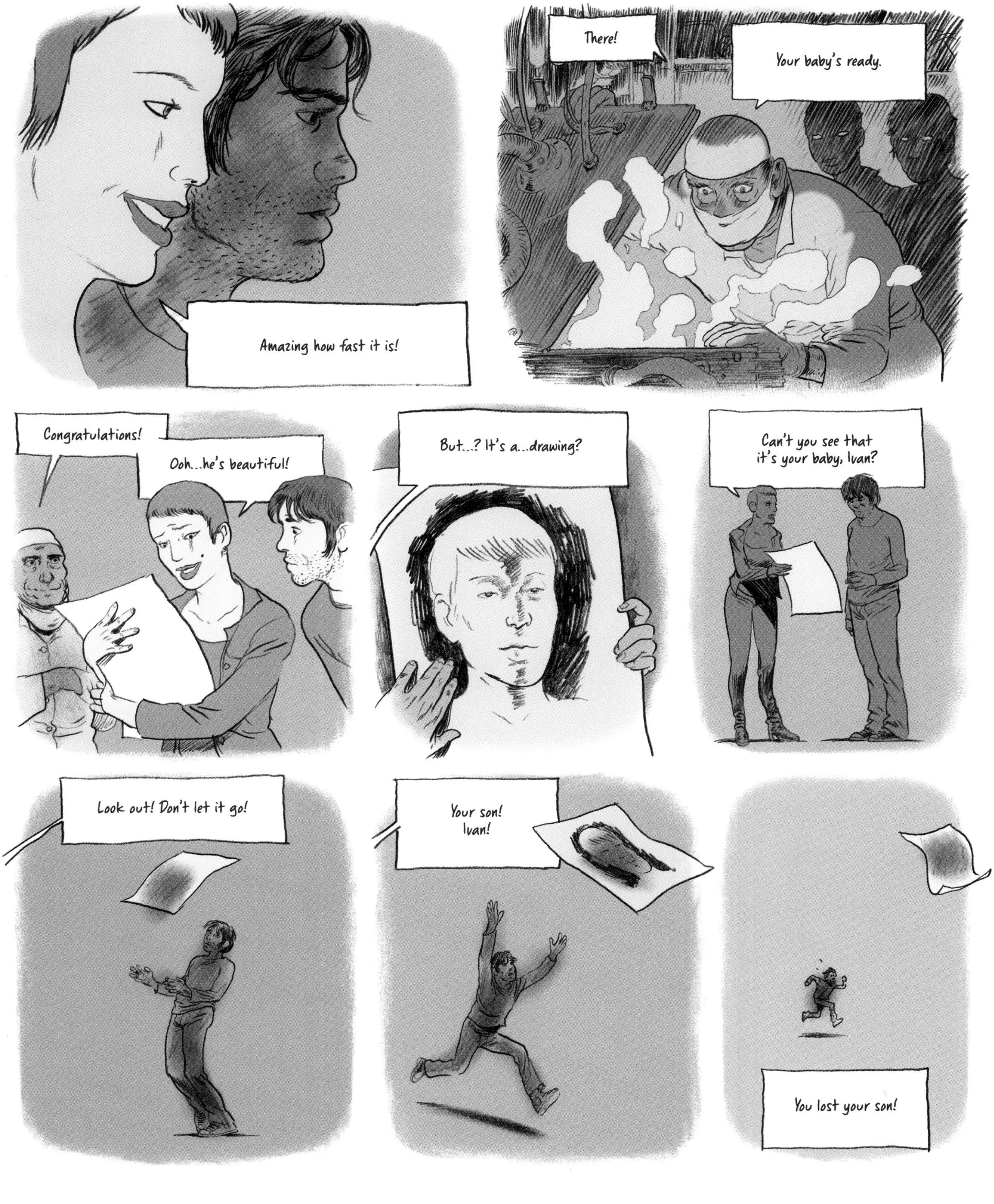

Amazing how fast it is!
There!
Your baby's ready.
Congratulations!
Ooh...he's beautiful!
But...? It's a...drawing?
Can't you see that it's your baby, Ivan?
Look out! Don't let it go!
Your son! Ivan!
You lost your son!

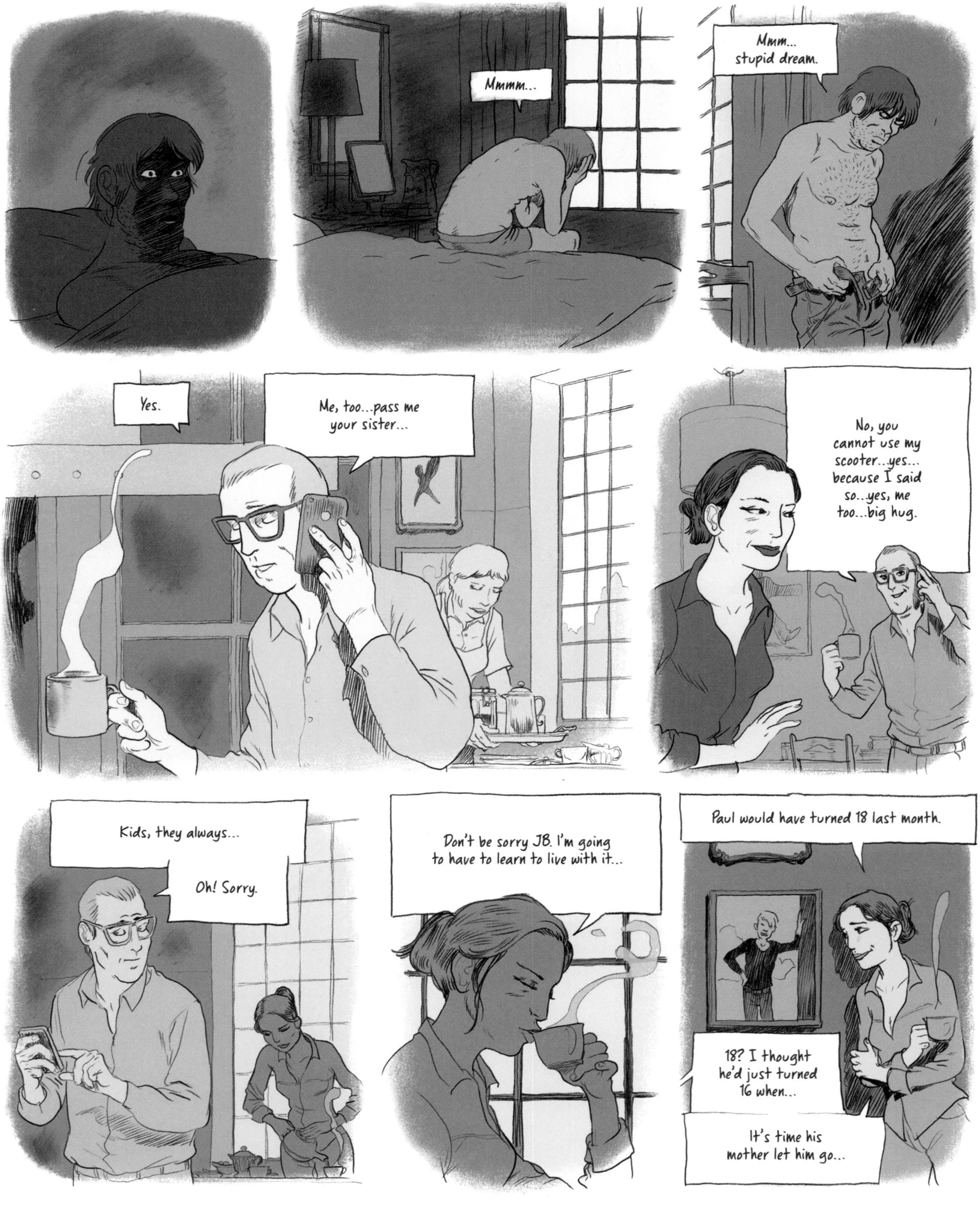
Mmmm...
Mmm... stupid dream.
Yes.
Me, too...pass me your sister...
No, you cannot use my scooter...yes... because I said so...yes, me too...big hug.
Kids, they always...
Oh! Sorry.
Don't be sorry JB. I'm going to have to learn to live with it...
Paul would have turned 18 last month.
18? I thought he'd just turned 16 when...
It's time his mother let him go...

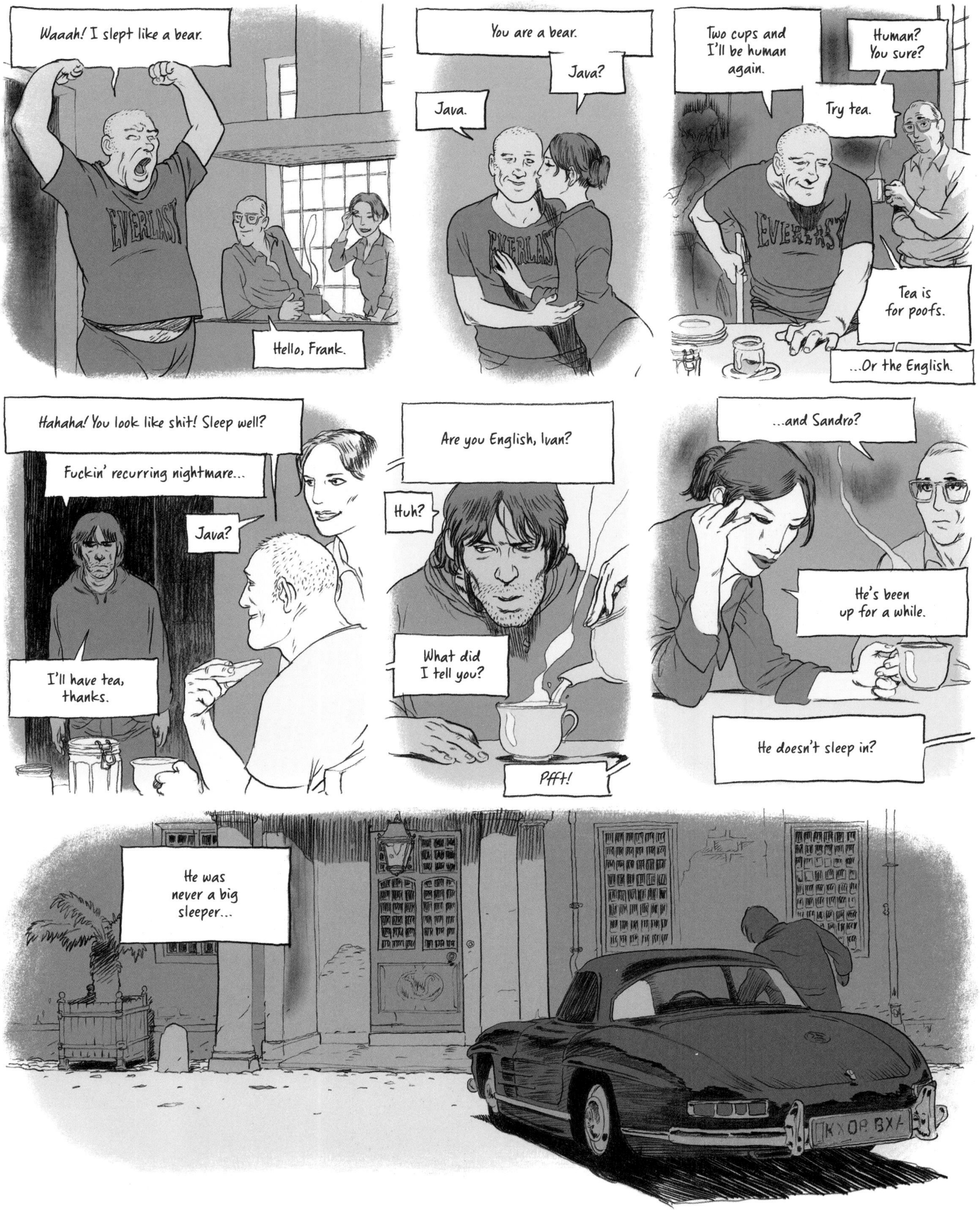

Waaah! I slept like a bear.
Hello, Frank.
You are a bear.
Java?
Java.
Two cups and I'll be human again.
Human? You sure?
Try tea.
Tea is for poofs.
...Or the English.
Hahaha! You look like shit! Sleep well?
Fuckin' recurring nightmare...
Java?
I'll have tea, thanks.
Are you English, Ivan?
Huh?
What did I tell you?
Pfft!
...and Sandro?
He's been up for a while.
He doesn't sleep in?
He was never a big sleeper...

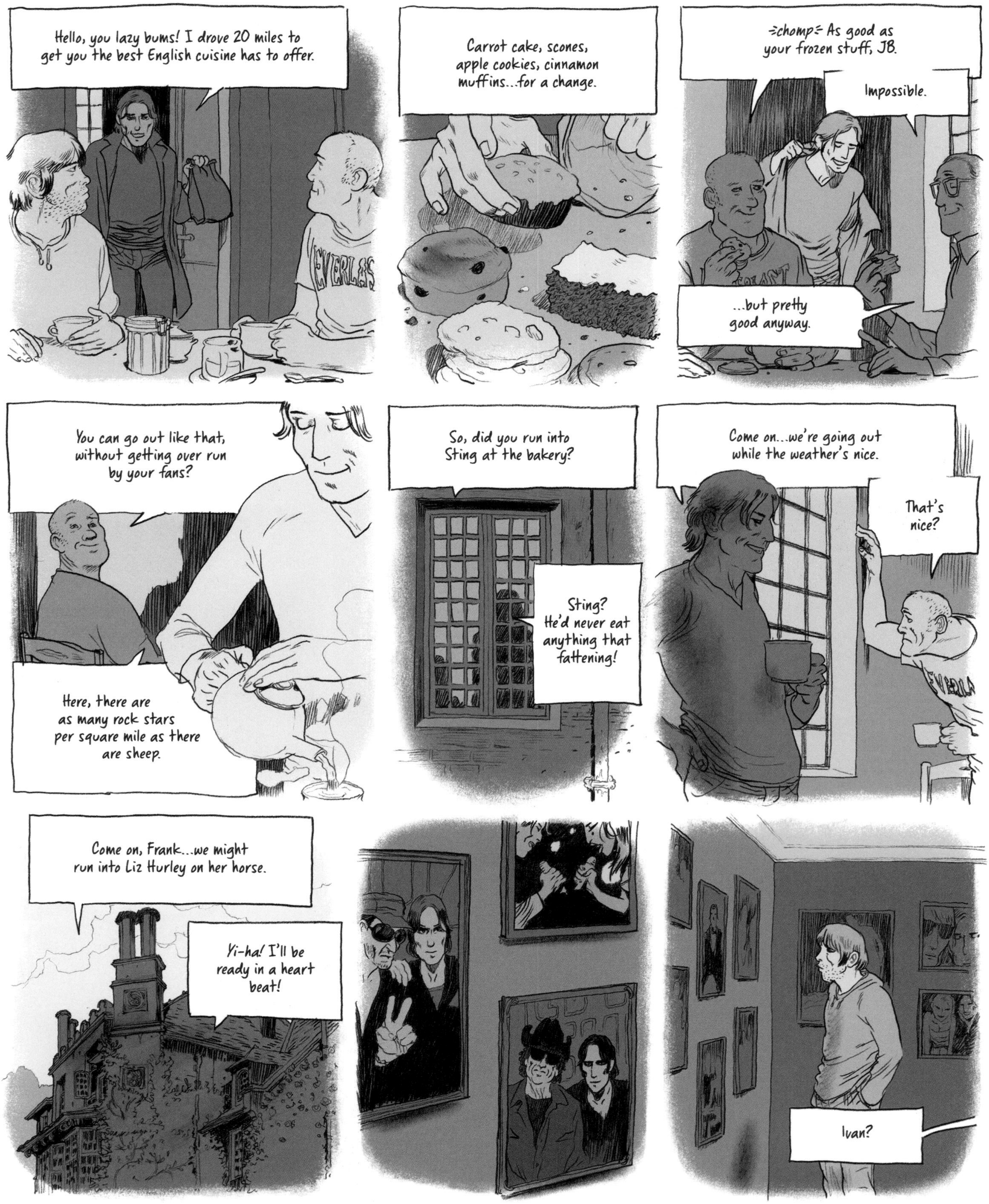
Hello, you lazy bums! I drove 20 miles to get you the best English cuisine has to offer.
Carrot cake, scones, apple cookies, cinnamon muffins...for a change.
=chomp= As good as your frozen stuff, JB.
Impossible.
...but pretty good anyway.
You can go out like that, without getting over run by your fans?
Here, there are as many rock stars per square mile as there are sheep.
So, did you run into Sting at the bakery?
Sting? He'd never eat anything that fattening!
Come on...we're going out while the weather's nice.
That's nice?
Come on, Frank...we might run into Liz Hurley on her horse.
Yi-ha! I'll be ready in a heart beat!
Ivan?

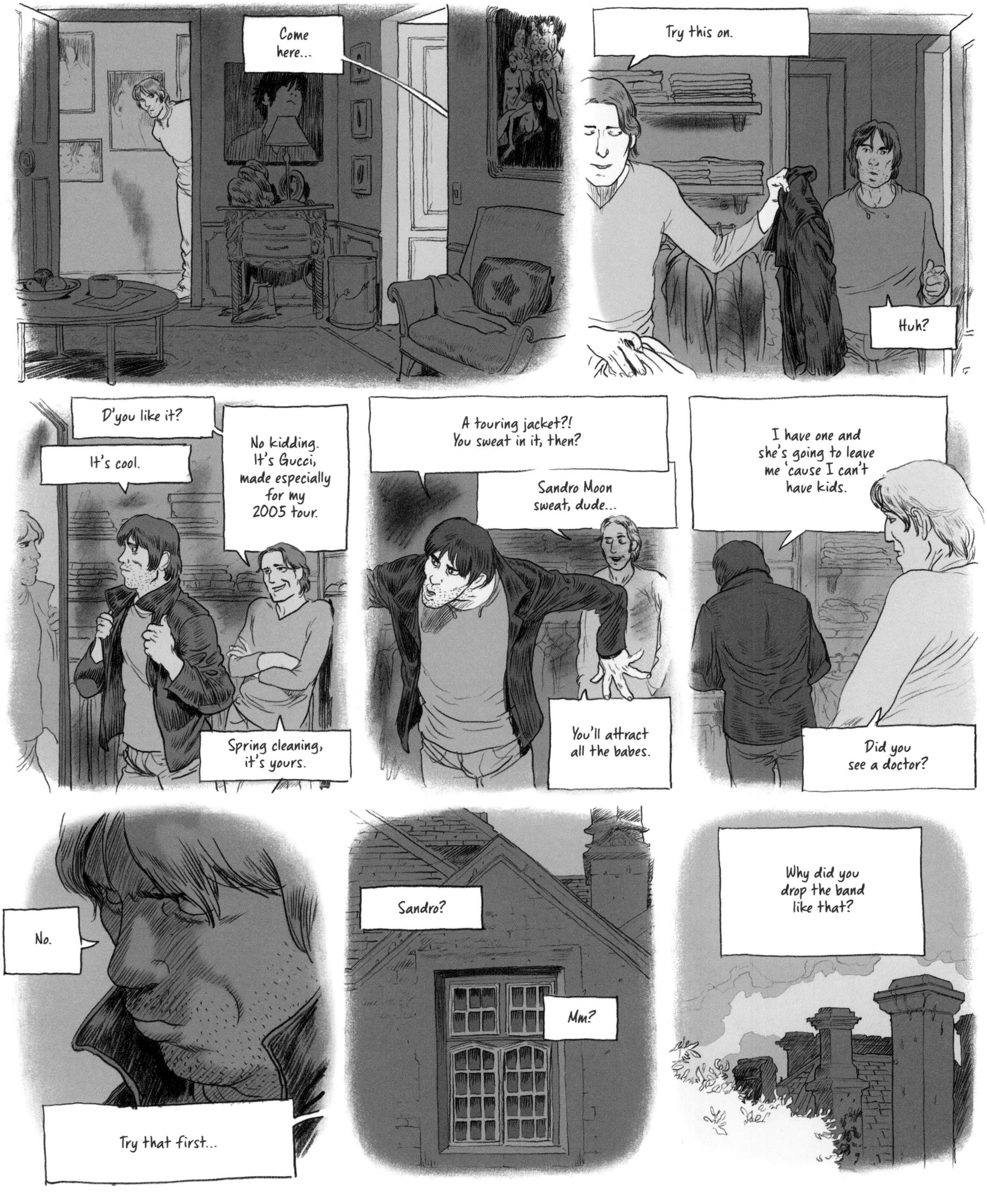
Come here...
Try this on.
Huh?
D'you like it?
It's cool.
No kidding. It's Gucci, made especially for my 2005 tour.
Spring cleaning, it's yours.
A touring jacket?! You sweat in it, then?
Sandro Moon sweat, dude...
You'll attract all the babes.
I have one and she's going to leave me 'cause I can't have kids.
Did you see a doctor?
No.
Try that first...
Sandro?
Mm?
Why did you drop the band like that?

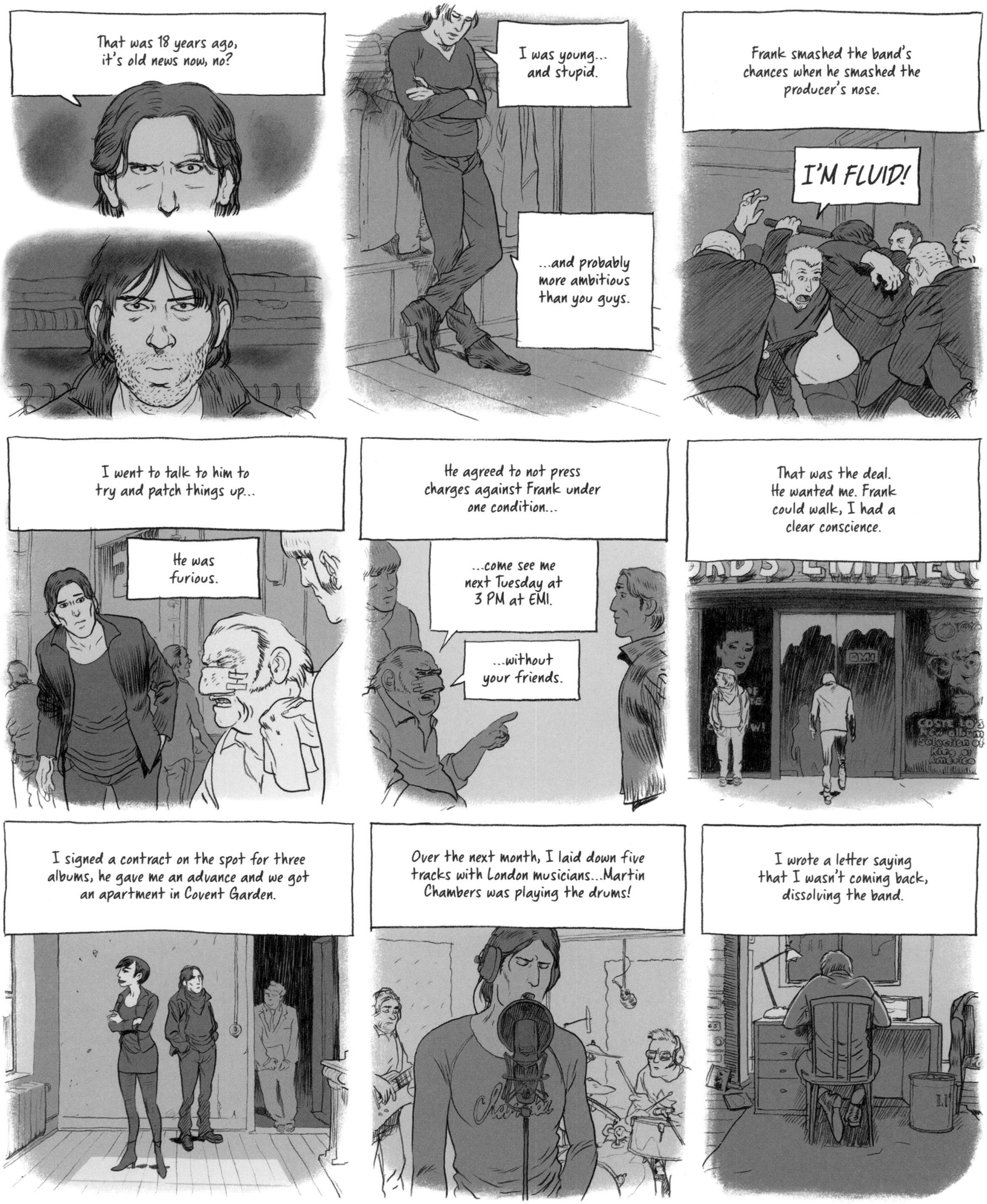
That was 18 years ago, it's old news now, no?
I was young... and stupid.
...and probably more ambitious than you guys.
Frank smashed the band's chances when he smashed the producer's nose.
I'M FLUID!
I went to talk to him to try and patch things up...
He was furious.
He agreed to not press charges against Frank under one condition...
...come see me next Tuesday at 3 PM at EMI.
...without your friends.
That was the deal. He wanted me. Frank could walk, I had a clear conscience.
I signed a contract on the spot for three albums, he gave me an advance and we got an apartment in Covent Garden.
Over the next month, I laid down five tracks with London musicians...Martin Chambers was playing the drums!
I wrote a letter saying that I wasn't coming back, dissolving the band.

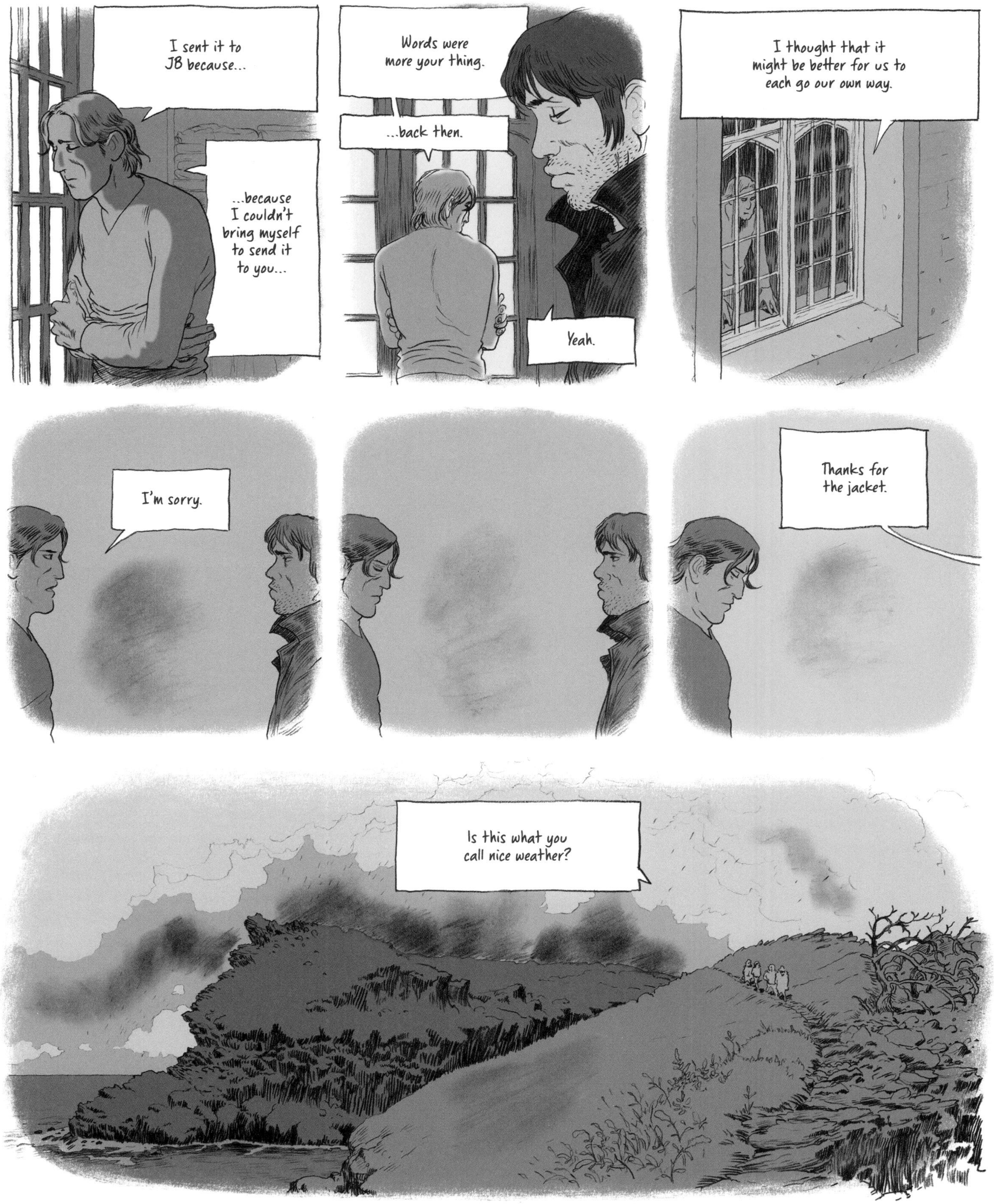
I sent it to JB because...
...because I couldn't bring myself to send it to you...
Words were more your thing.
...back then.
Yeah.
I thought that it might be better for us to each go our own way.
I'm sorry.
Thanks for the jacket.
Is this what you call nice weather?

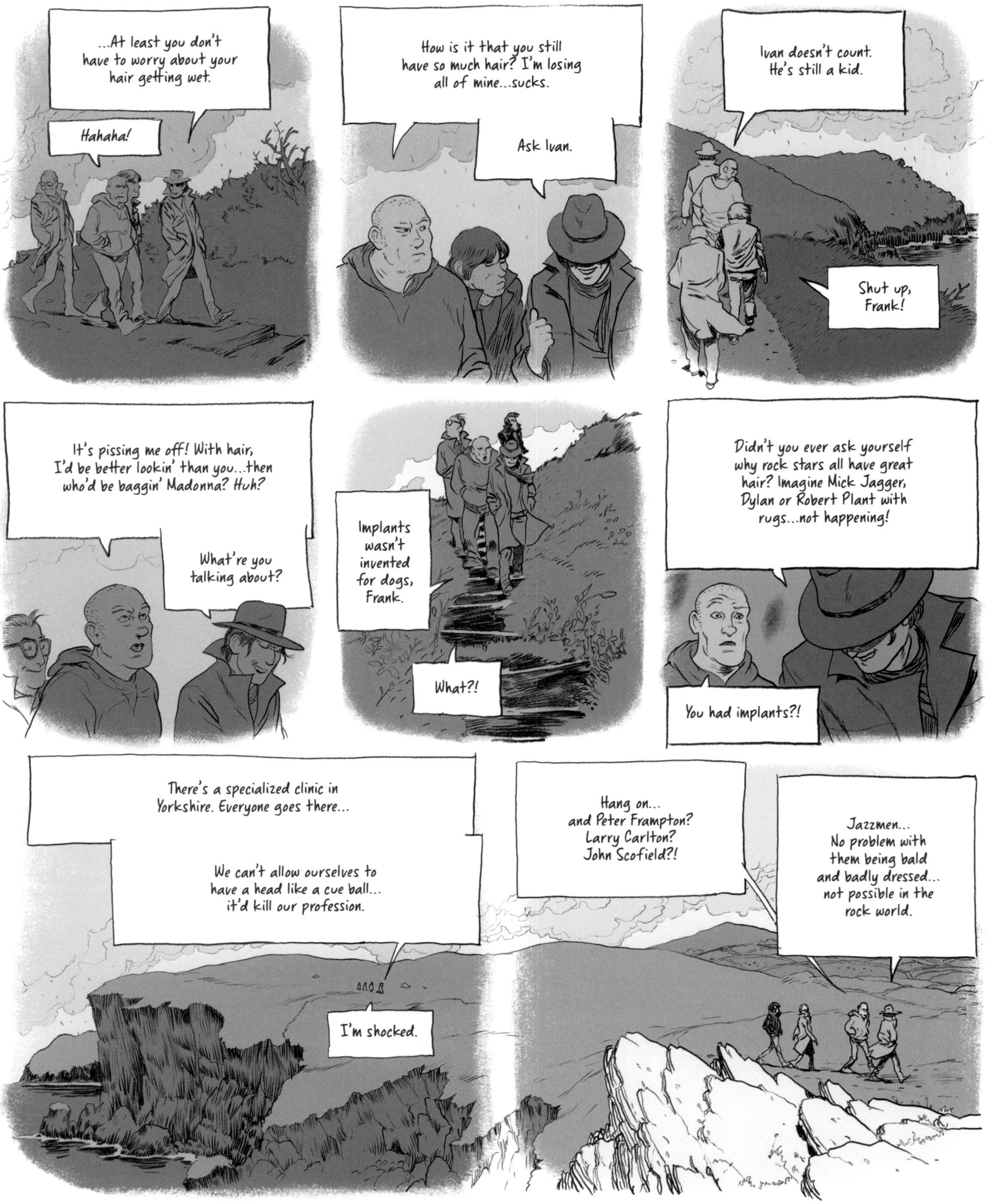
...At least you don't have to worry about your hair getting wet.
Hahaha!
How is it that you still have so much hair? I'm losing all of mine...sucks.
Ask Ivan.
Ivan doesn't count. He's still a kid.
Shut up, Frank!
It's pissing me off! With hair, I'd be better lookin' than you...then who'd be baggin' Madonna? Huh?
What're you talking about?
Implants wasn't invented for dogs, Frank.
What?!
Didn't you ever ask yourself why rock stars all have great hair? Imagine Mick Jagger, Dylan or Robert Plant with rugs...not happening!
You had implants?!
There's a specialized clinic in Yorkshire. Everyone goes there...
We can't allow ourselves to have a head like a cue ball... it'd kill our profession.
I'm shocked.
Hang on... and Peter Frampton? Larry Carlton? John Scofield?!
Jazzmen... No problem with them being bald and badly dressed... not possible in the rock world.

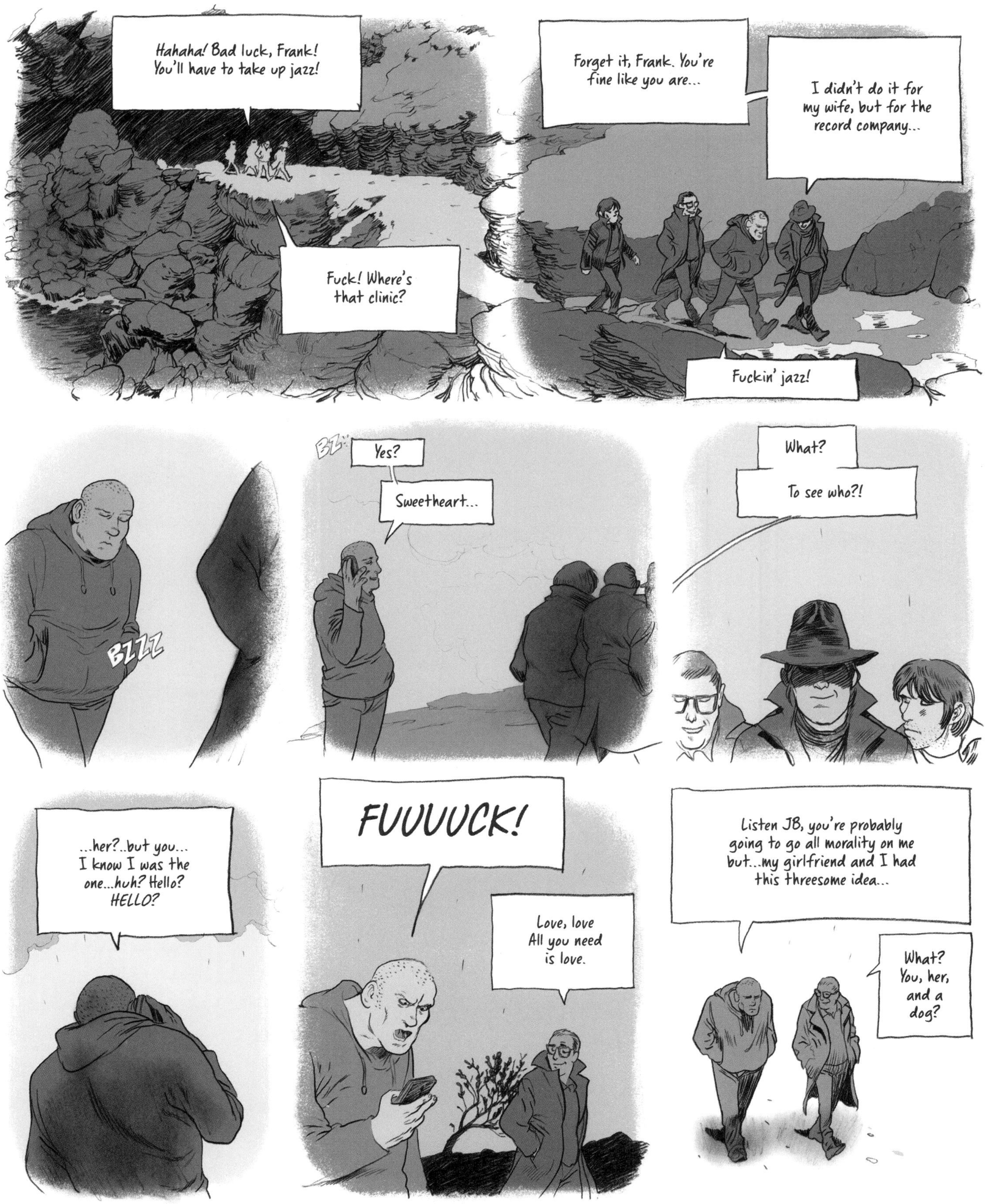
Hahaha! Bad luck, Frank! You'll have to take up jazz!
Fuck! Where's that clinic?
Forget it, Frank. You're fine like you are...
I didn't do it for my wife, but for the record company...
Fuckin' jazz!
BZZZ
BZ
Yes?
Sweetheart...
What?
To see who?!
...her?..but you... I know I was the one...huh? Hello? HELLO?
FUUUUCK!
Love, love All you need is love.
Listen JB, you're probably going to go all morality on me but...my girlfriend and I had this threesome idea...
What? You, her, and a dog?

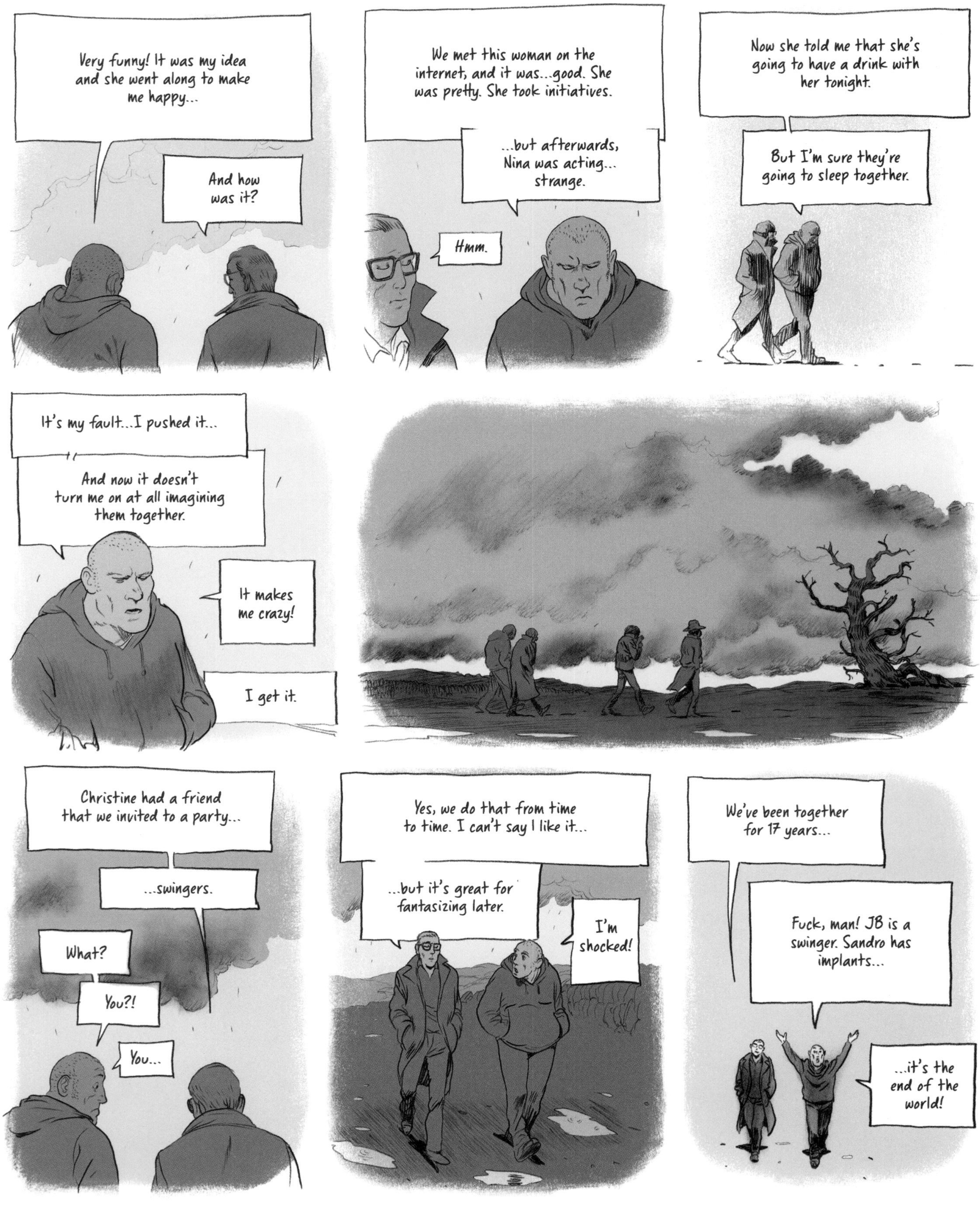

Very funny! It was my idea and she went along to make me happy...
And how was it?
We met this woman on the internet, and it was...good. She was pretty. She took initiatives.
...but afterwards, Nina was acting... strange.
Hmm.
Now she told me that she's going to have a drink with her tonight.
But I'm sure they're going to sleep together.
It's my fault...I pushed it...
And now it doesn't turn me on at all imagining them together.
It makes me crazy!
I get it.
Christine had a friend that we invited to a party...
...swingers.
What?
You?!
You...
Yes, we do that from time to time. I can't say I like it...
...but it's great for fantasizing later.
I'm shocked!
We've been together for 17 years...
Fuck, man! JB is a swinger. Sandro has implants...
...it's the end of the world!

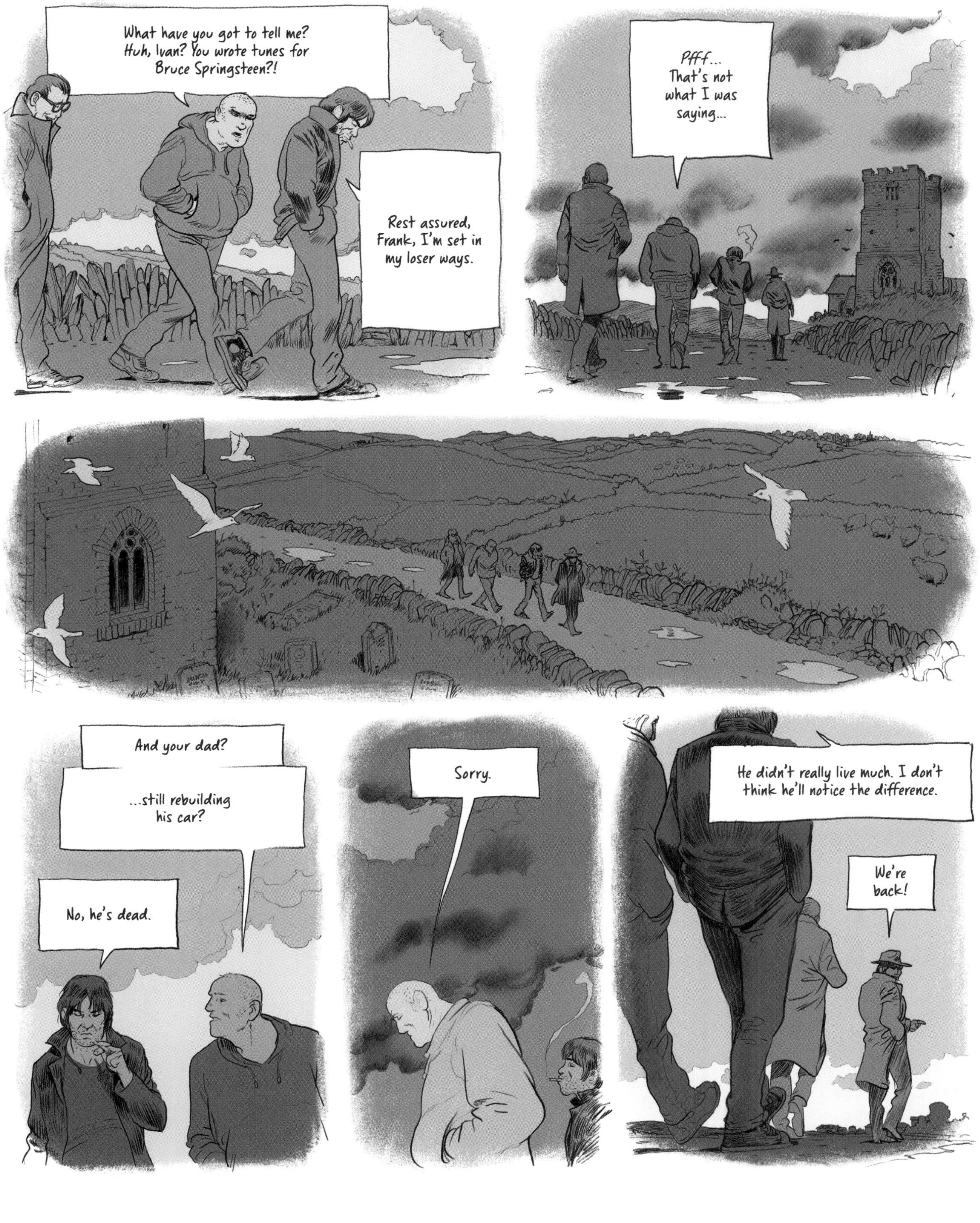
What have you got to tell me? Huh, Ivan? You wrote tunes for Bruce Springsteen?!
Rest assured, Frank, I'm set in my loser ways.
Pfff... That's not what I was saying...
And your dad?
...still rebuilding his car?
No, he's dead.
Sorry.
He didn't really live much. I don't think he'll notice the difference.
We're back!

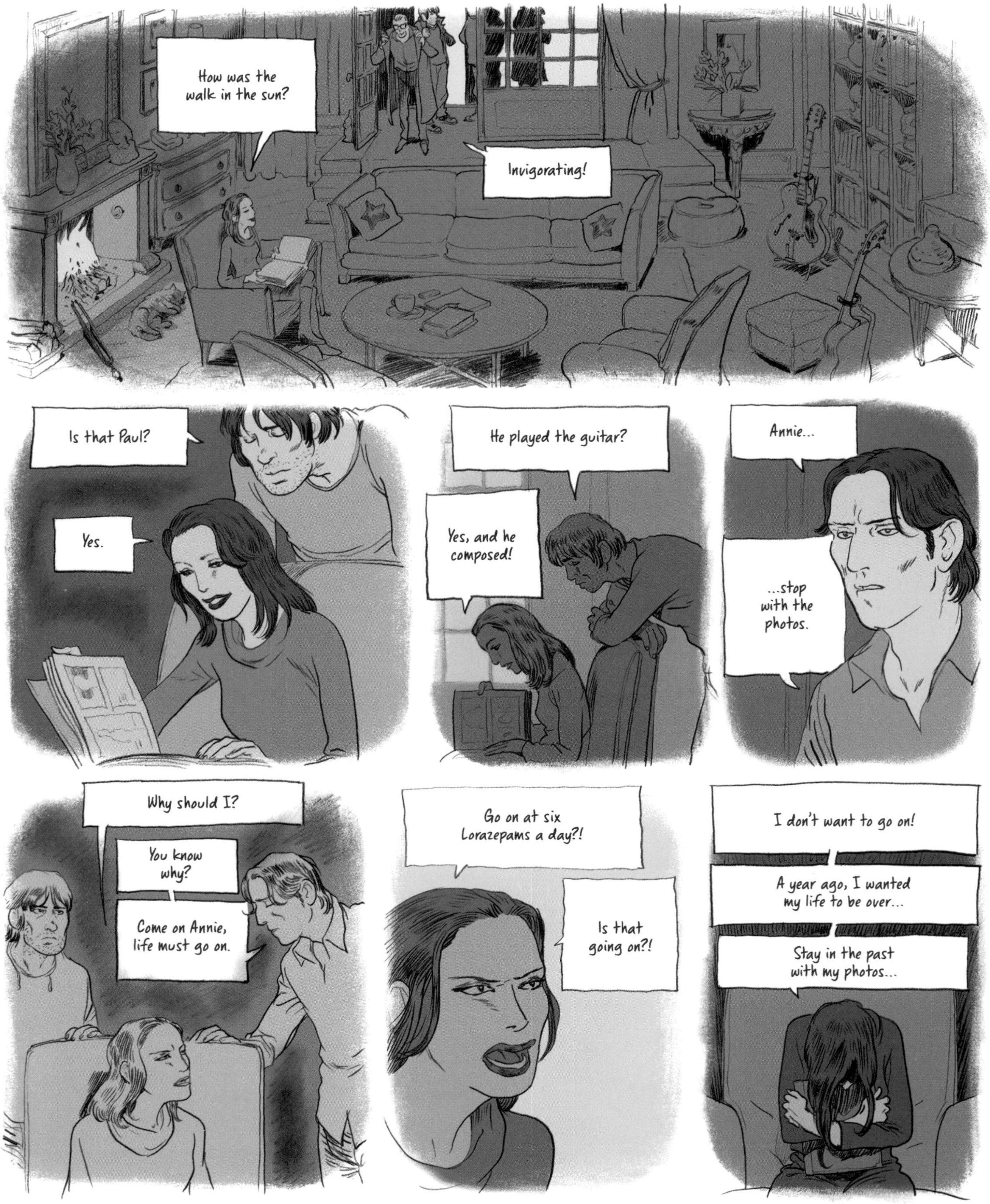
How was the walk in the sun?
Invigorating!
Is that Paul?
Yes.
He played the guitar?
Yes, and he composed!
Annie...
...stop with the photos.
Why should I?
You know why?
Come on Annie, life must go on.
Go on at six Lorazepams a day?!
Is that going on?!
I don't want to go on!
A year ago, I wanted my life to be over...
Stay in the past with my photos...

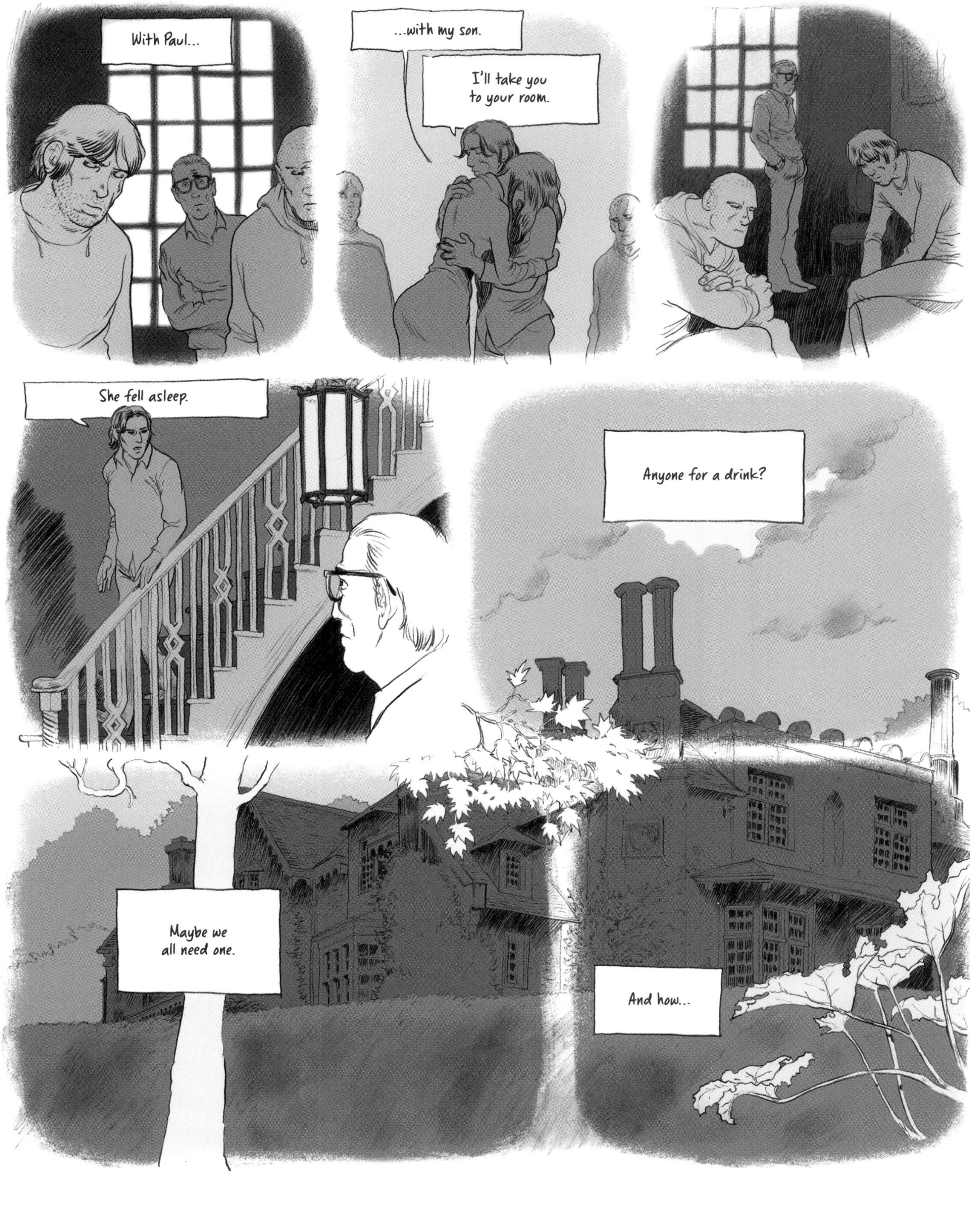
With Paul...
...with my son.
I'll take you to your room.
She fell asleep.
Anyone for a drink?
Maybe we all need one.
And how...

Mmm...

Now that's whiskey!

How is it that people who can make something like this, drink tea?!

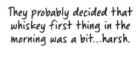

They probably decided that whiskey first thing in the morning was a bit...harsh.

Pussies.

Uh...and why is it exactly that you brought us all together, Sandro?

Because I thought it would be good to see you guys... ⸗weee⸗ ...and I thought it would be good for Annie...

That's all?

What? You thought I wanted forgiveness for becoming a rock star while you guys had your little lives?

Stop, will you! Rock was my scene, not yours!

And, may I remind you, I wasn't the one that took down the band, it was Frank.

Whoa, dude. I just broke some BBC guy's nose.

You were the one that left the band...and it was a good thing!

Look what you became... and look at how handsome we all are.

A bit bald, but hey...

Shut up, Ivan.

I wasn't talking about that Sandro...

The band, for me, is just some great memories, that's all... I could not of had a career like yours...

I'm not bitter.

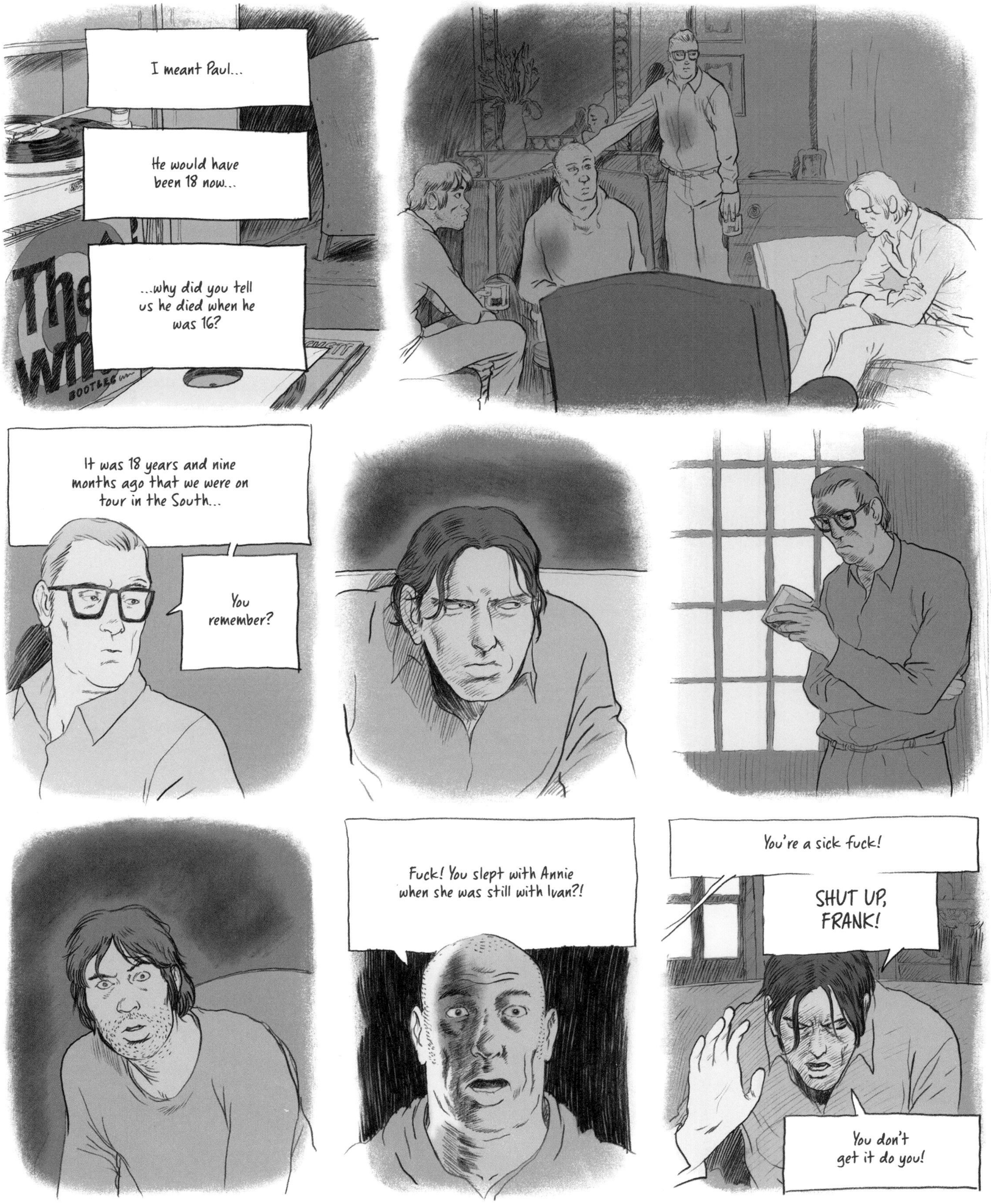
I meant Paul...
He would have been 18 now...
...why did you tell us he died when he was 16?
The Who
BOOTLEG
It was 18 years and nine months ago that we were on tour in the South...
You remember?
Fuck! You slept with Annie when she was still with Ivan?!
You're a sick fuck!
SHUT UP, FRANK!
You don't get it do you!

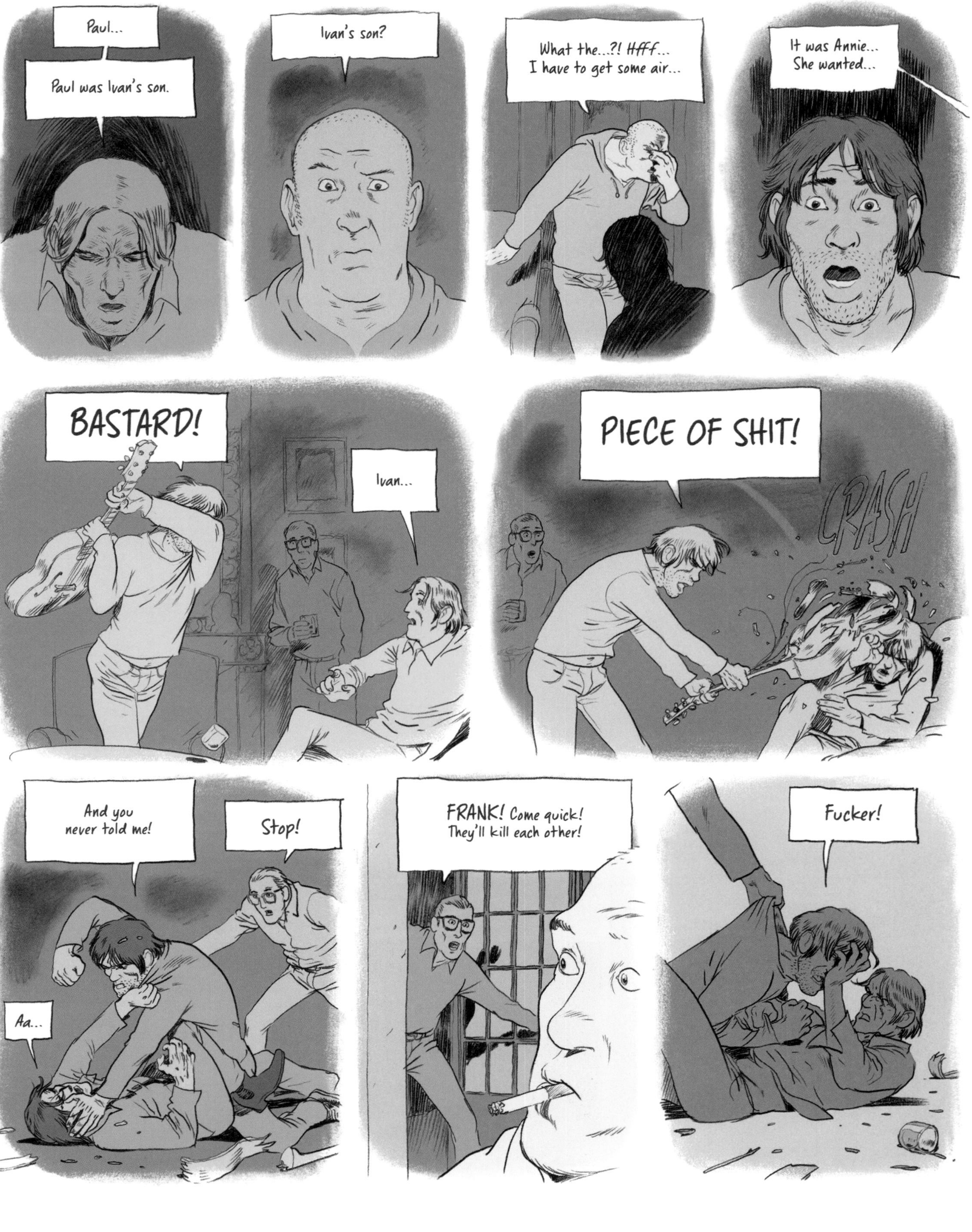
Paul...
Paul was Ivan's son.
Ivan's son?
What the...?! Hfff...
I have to get some air...
It was Annie...
She wanted...
BASTARD!
Ivan...
PIECE OF SHIT!
CRASH
And you never told me!
Stop!
Aa...
FRANK! Come quick! They'll kill each other!
Fucker!

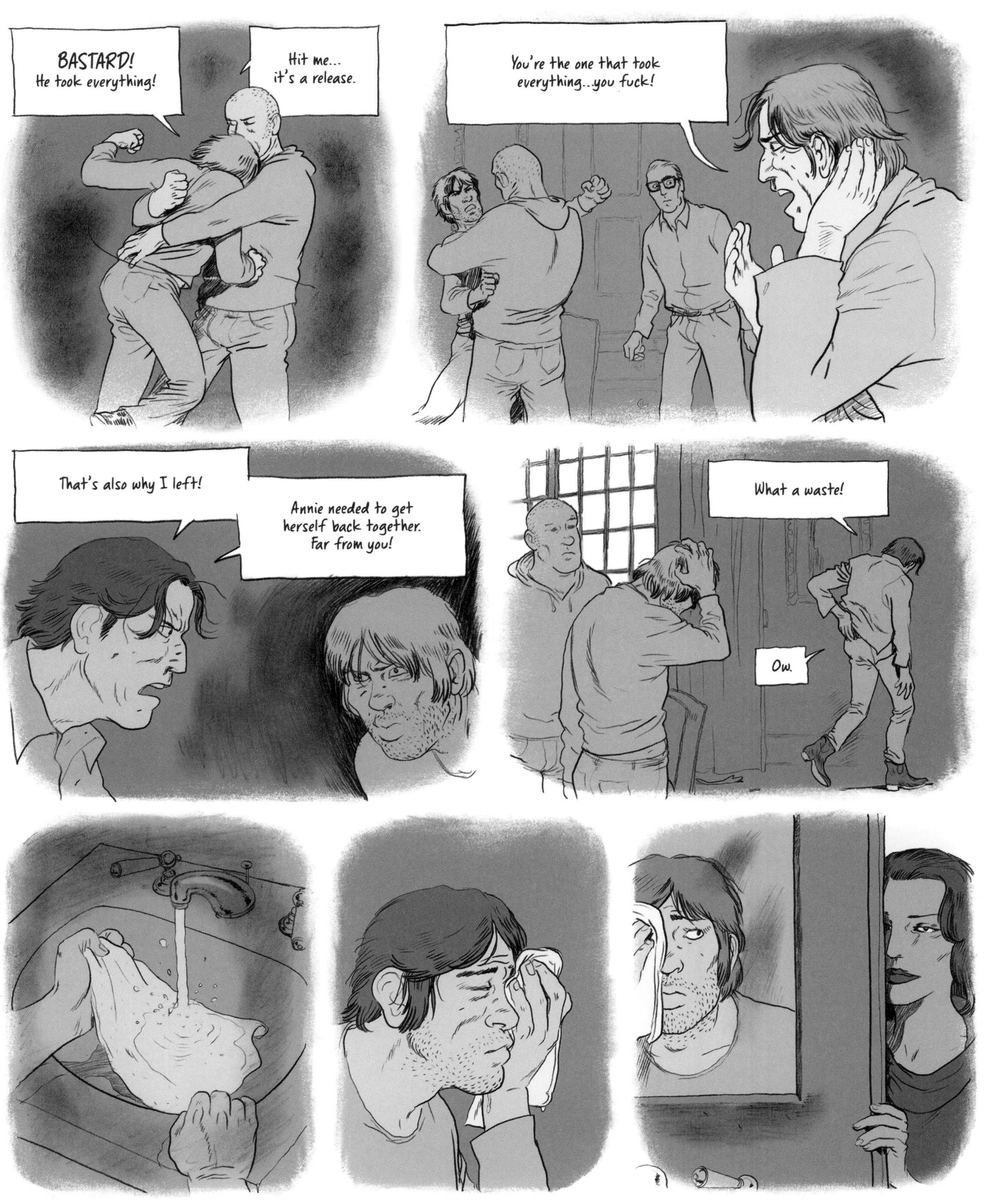
BASTARD!
He took everything!
Hit me...
it's a release.
You're the one that took
everything...you fuck!
That's also why I left!
Annie needed to get
herself back together.
Far from you!
What a waste!
Ow.

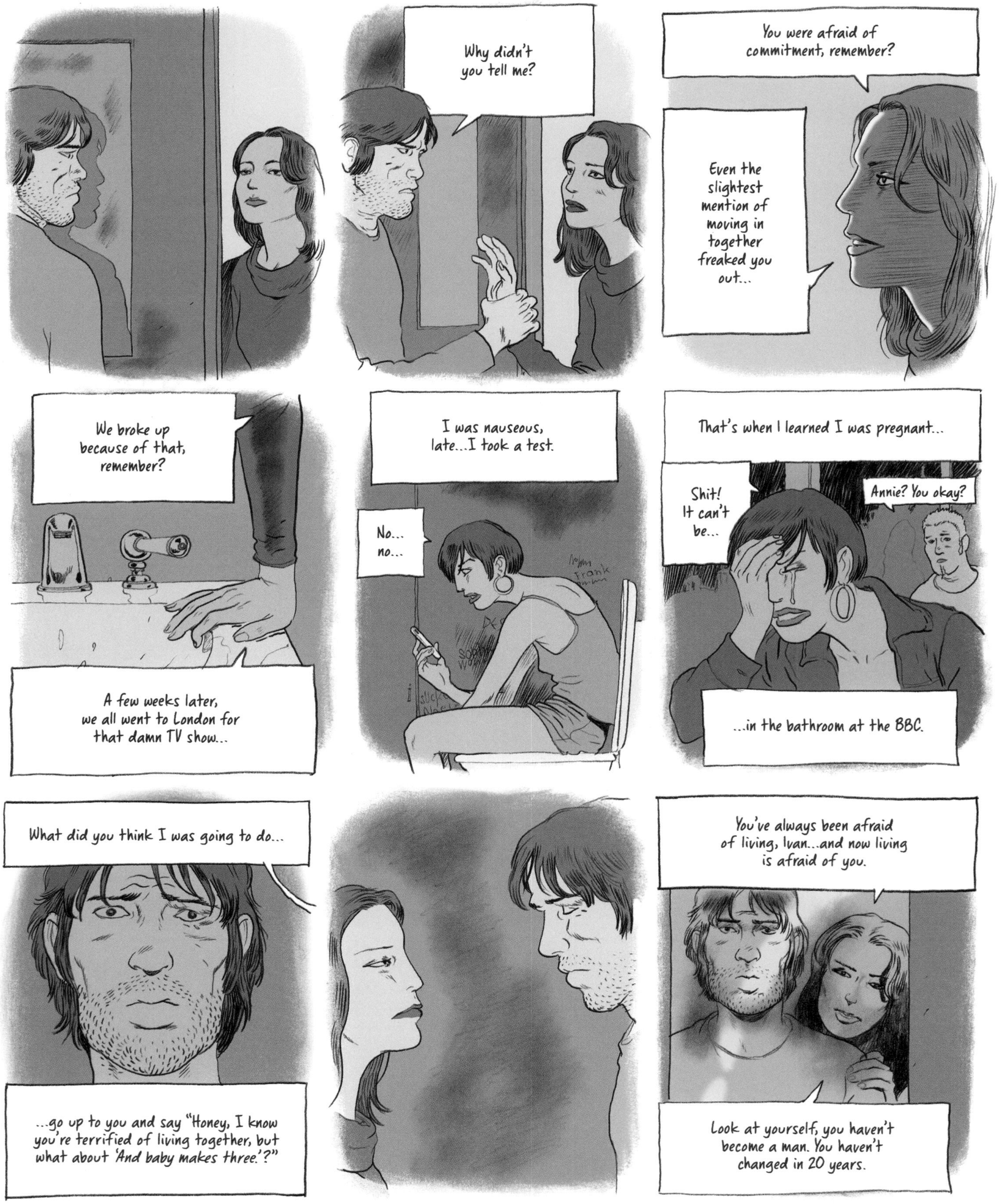

Why didn't you tell me?
You were afraid of commitment, remember?
Even the slightest mention of moving in together freaked you out...
We broke up because of that, remember?
A few weeks later, we all went to London for that damn TV show...
I was nauseous, late...I took a test.
No... no...
That's when I learned I was pregnant...
Shit! It can't be...
Annie? You okay?
...in the bathroom at the BBC.
What did you think I was going to do...
...go up to you and say "Honey, I know you're terrified of living together, but what about 'And baby makes three.'?"
You've always been afraid of living, Ivan...and now living is afraid of you.
Look at yourself, you haven't become a man. You haven't changed in 20 years.

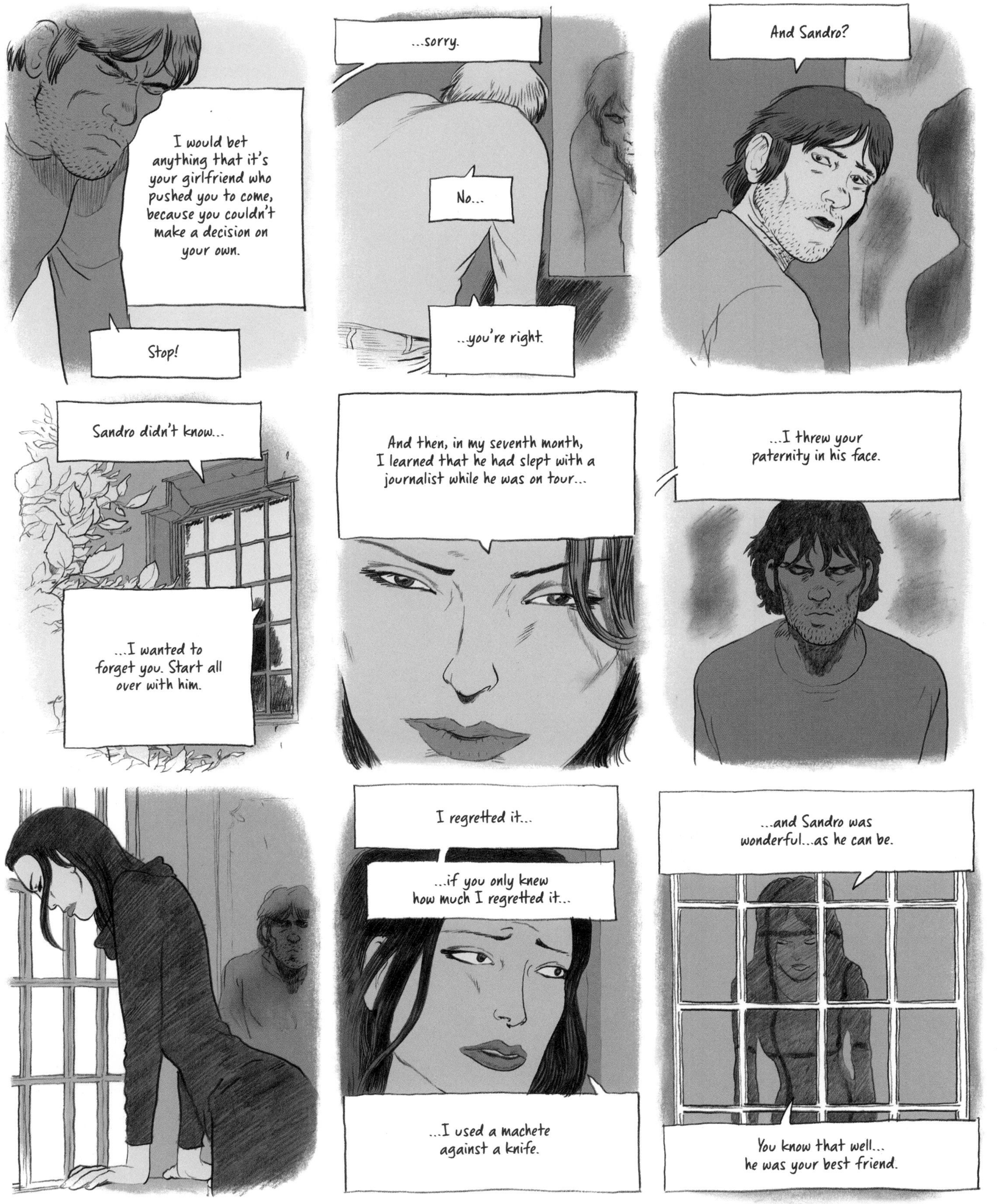
I would bet anything that it's your girlfriend who pushed you to come, because you couldn't make a decision on your own.
Stop!
...sorry.
No...
...you're right.
And Sandro?
Sandro didn't know...
...I wanted to forget you. Start all over with him.
And then, in my seventh month, I learned that he had slept with a journalist while he was on tour...
...I threw your paternity in his face.
I regretted it...
...if you only knew how much I regretted it...
...I used a machete against a knife.
...and Sandro was wonderful...as he can be.
You know that well... he was your best friend.

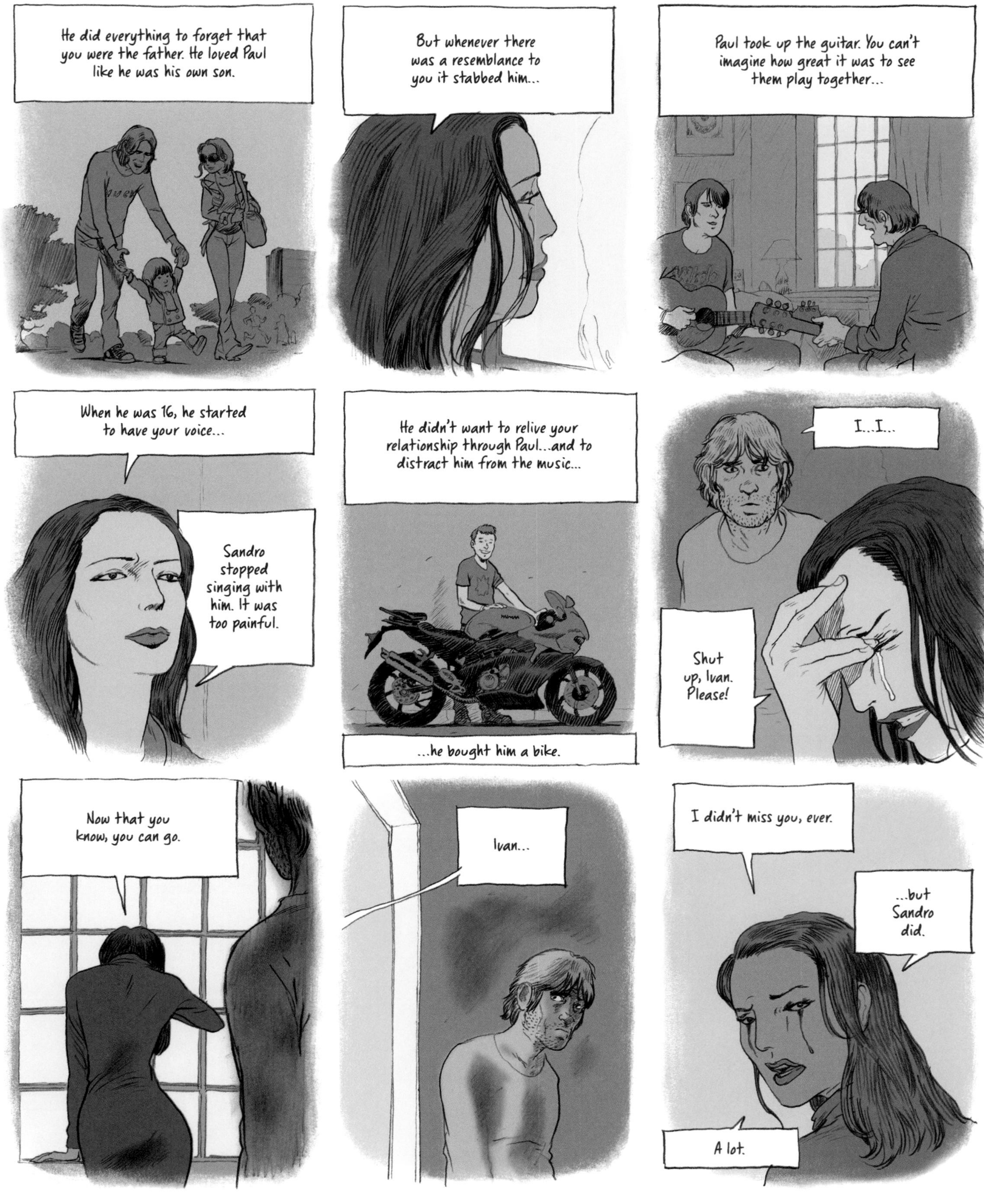
He did everything to forget that you were the father. He loved Paul like he was his own son.
But whenever there was a resemblance to you it stabbed him...
Paul took up the guitar. You can't imagine how great it was to see them play together...
When he was 16, he started to have your voice...
Sandro stopped singing with him. It was too painful.
He didn't want to relive your relationship through Paul...and to distract him from the music...
...he bought him a bike.
I...I...
Shut up, Ivan. Please!
Now that you know, you can go.
Ivan...
I didn't miss you, ever.
...but Sandro did.
A lot.

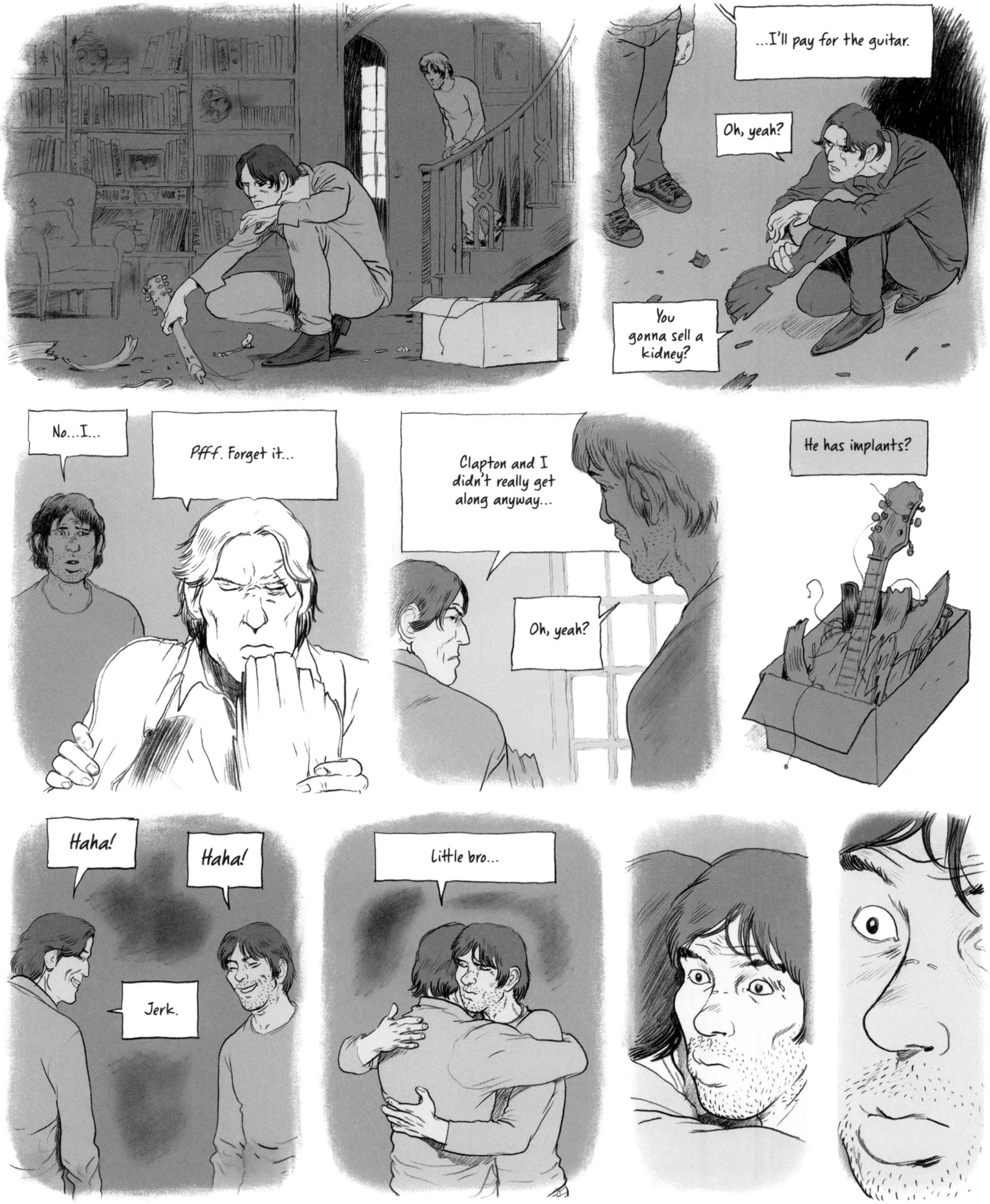
...I'll pay for the guitar.
Oh, yeah?
You gonna sell a kidney?
No...I...
Pfff. Forget it...
Clapton and I didn't really get along anyway...
Oh, yeah?
He has implants?
Haha!
Haha!
Jerk.
Little bro...

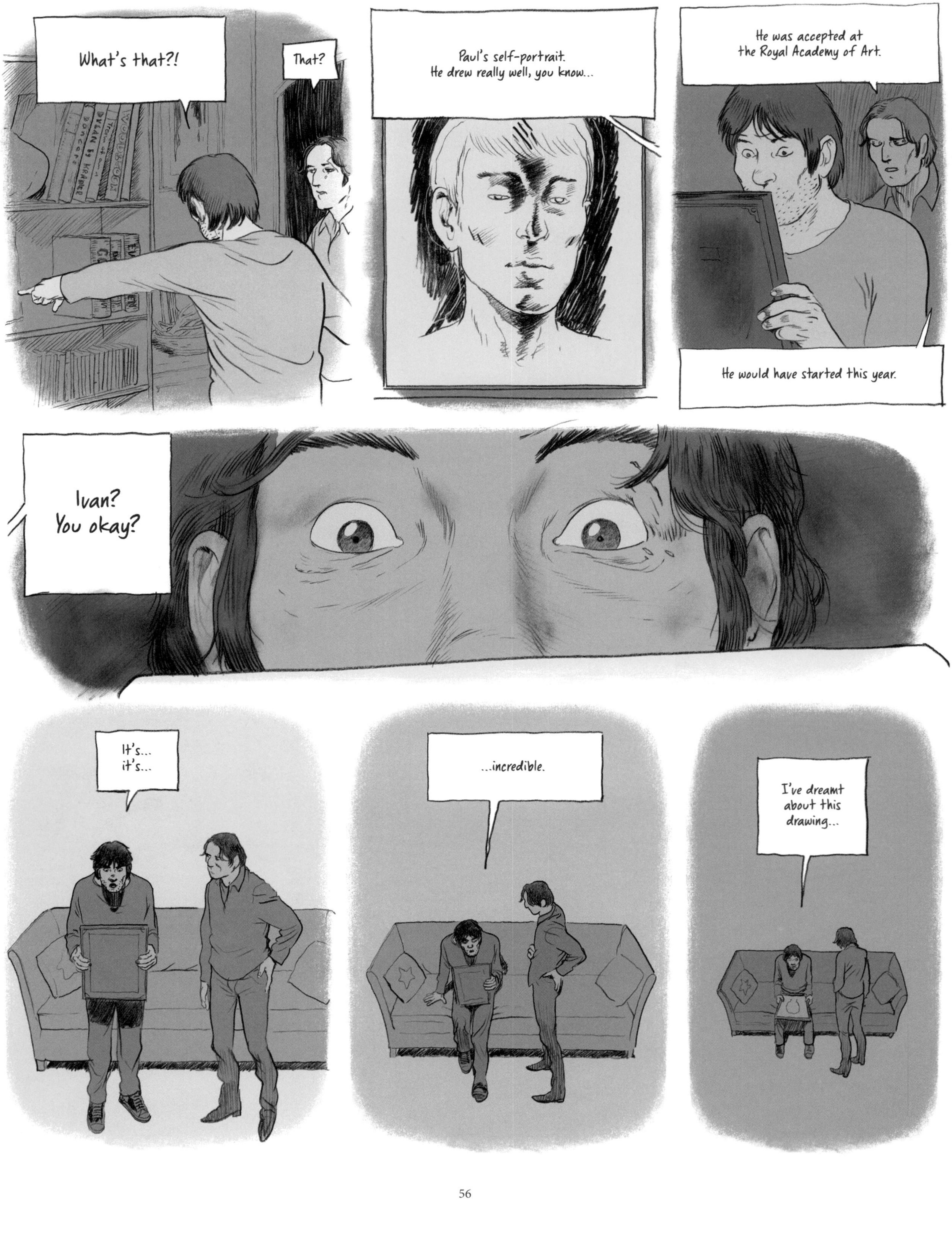
What's that?!
That?
Paul's self-portrait. He drew really well, you know...
He was accepted at the Royal Academy of Art.
He would have started this year.
Ivan? You okay?
It's... it's...
...incredible.
I've dreamt about this drawing...

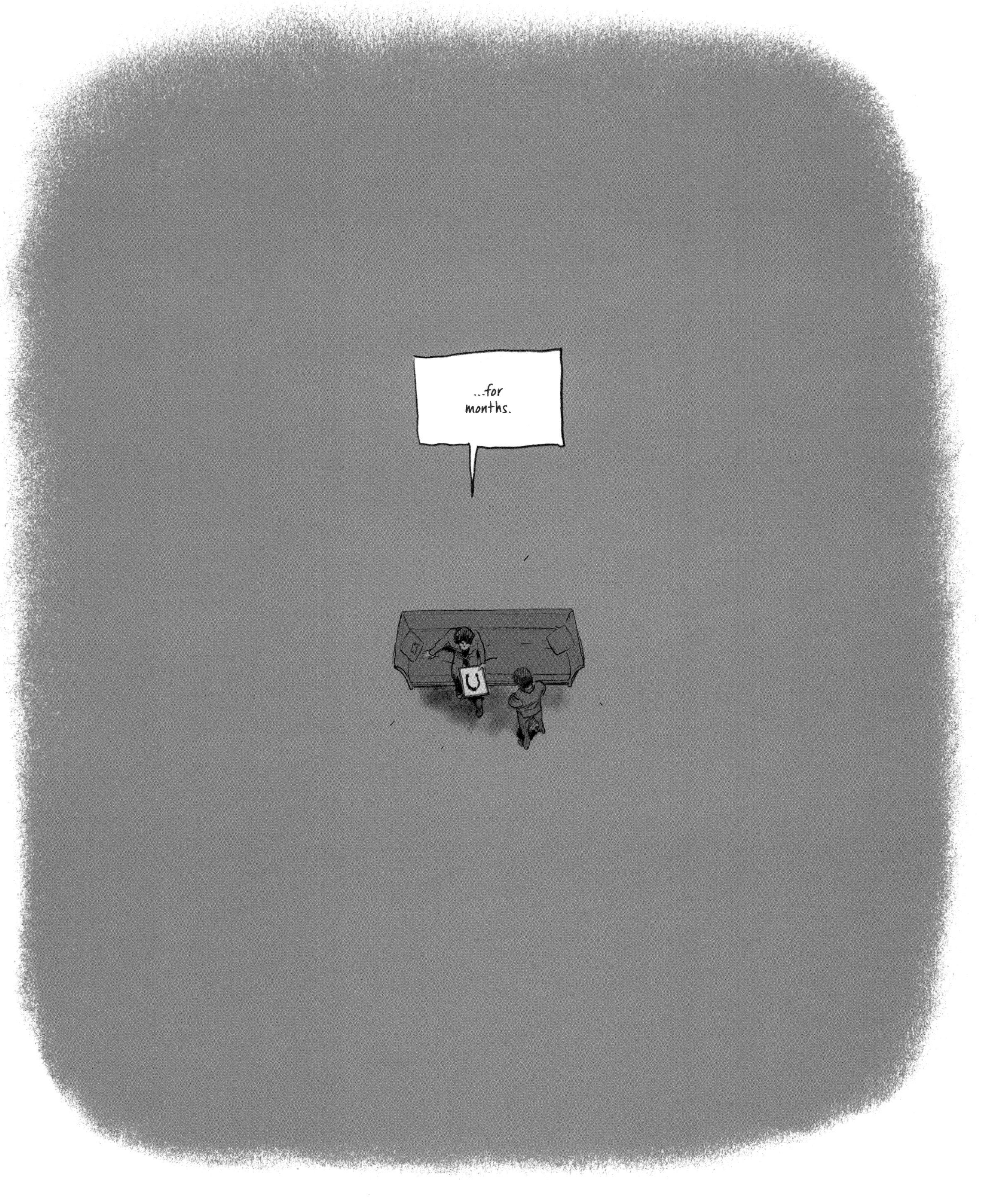
...for months.

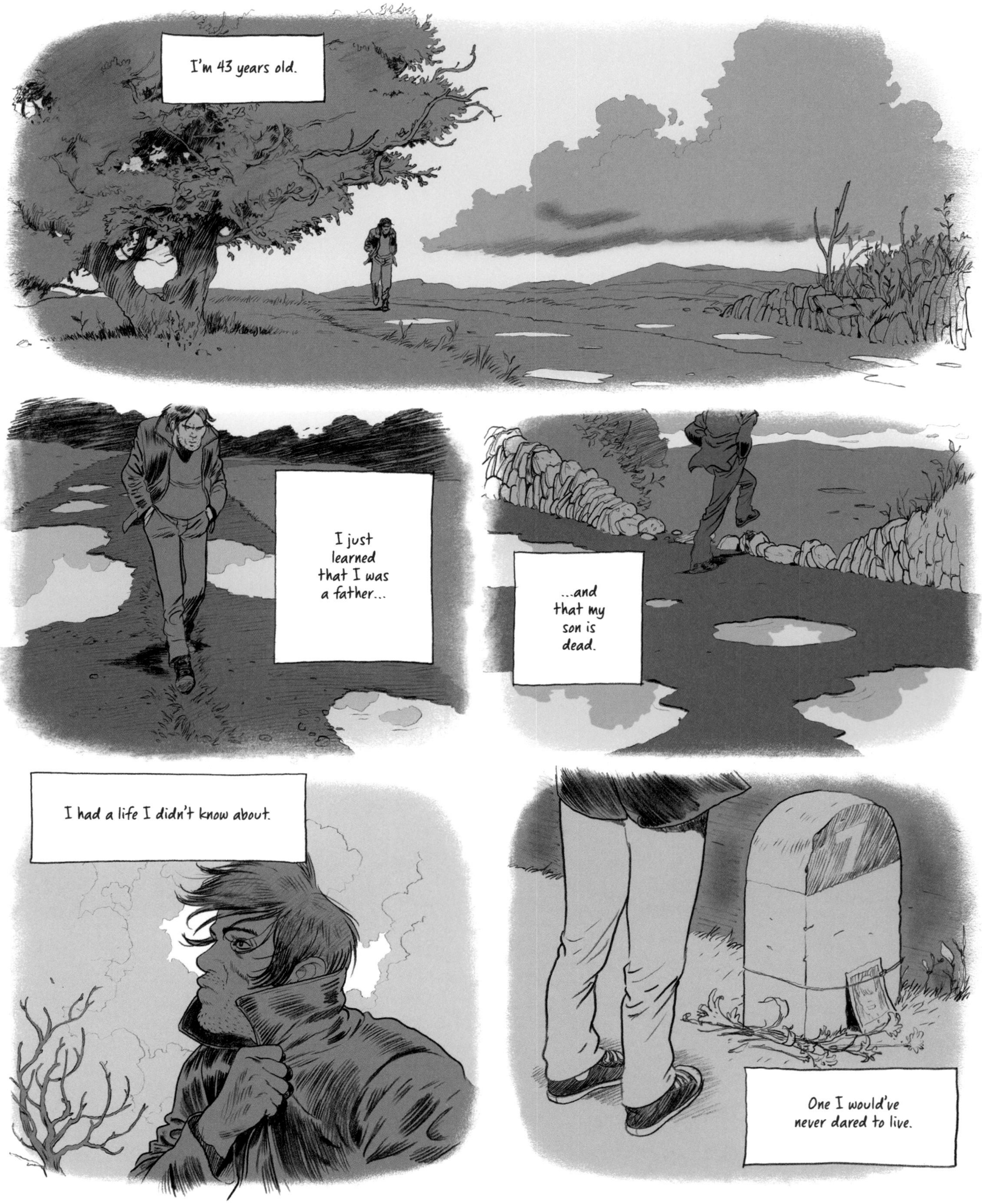
I'm 43 years old.
I just learned that I was a father...
...and that my son is dead.
I had a life I didn't know about.
One I would've never dared to live.

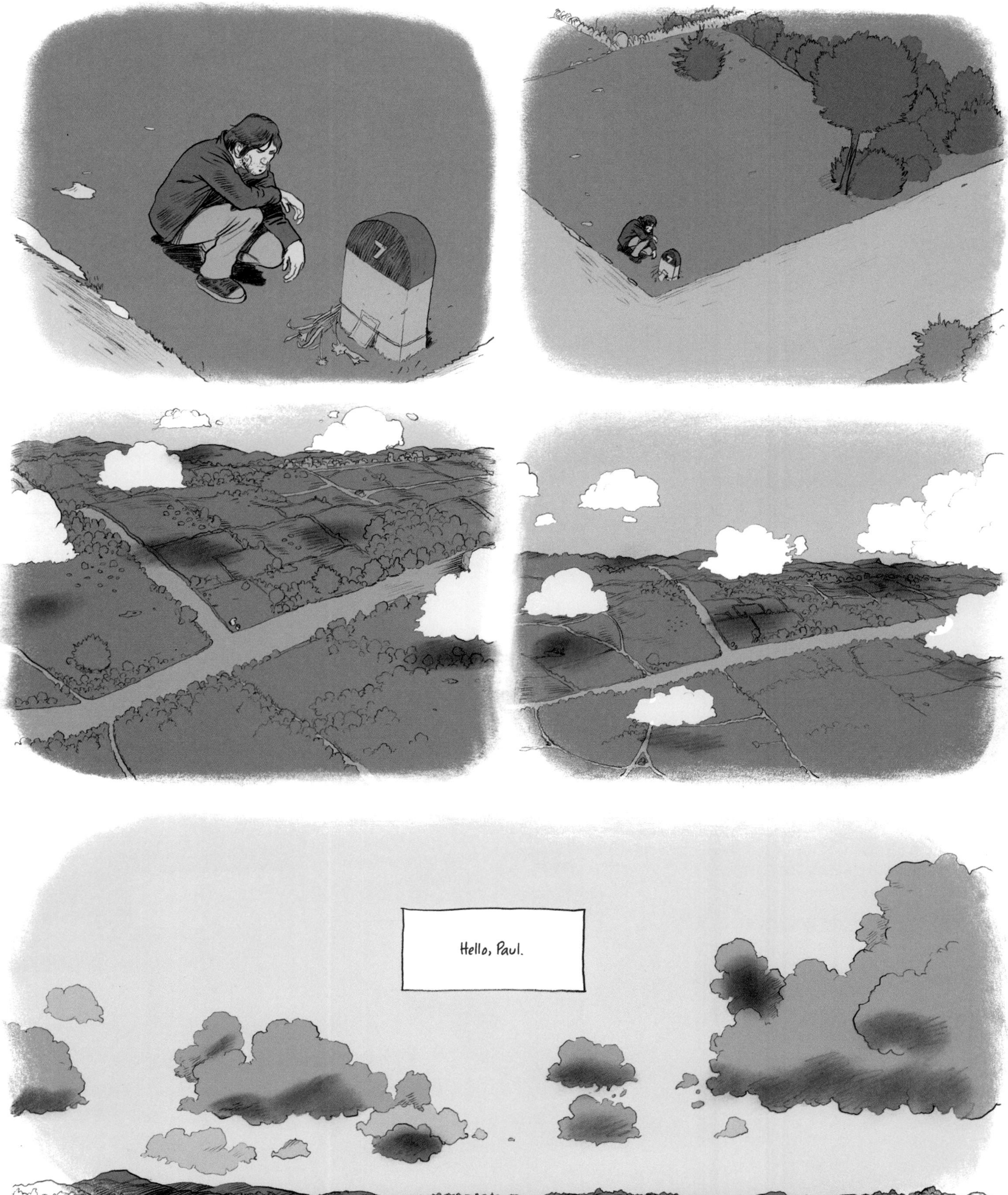
Hello, Paul.

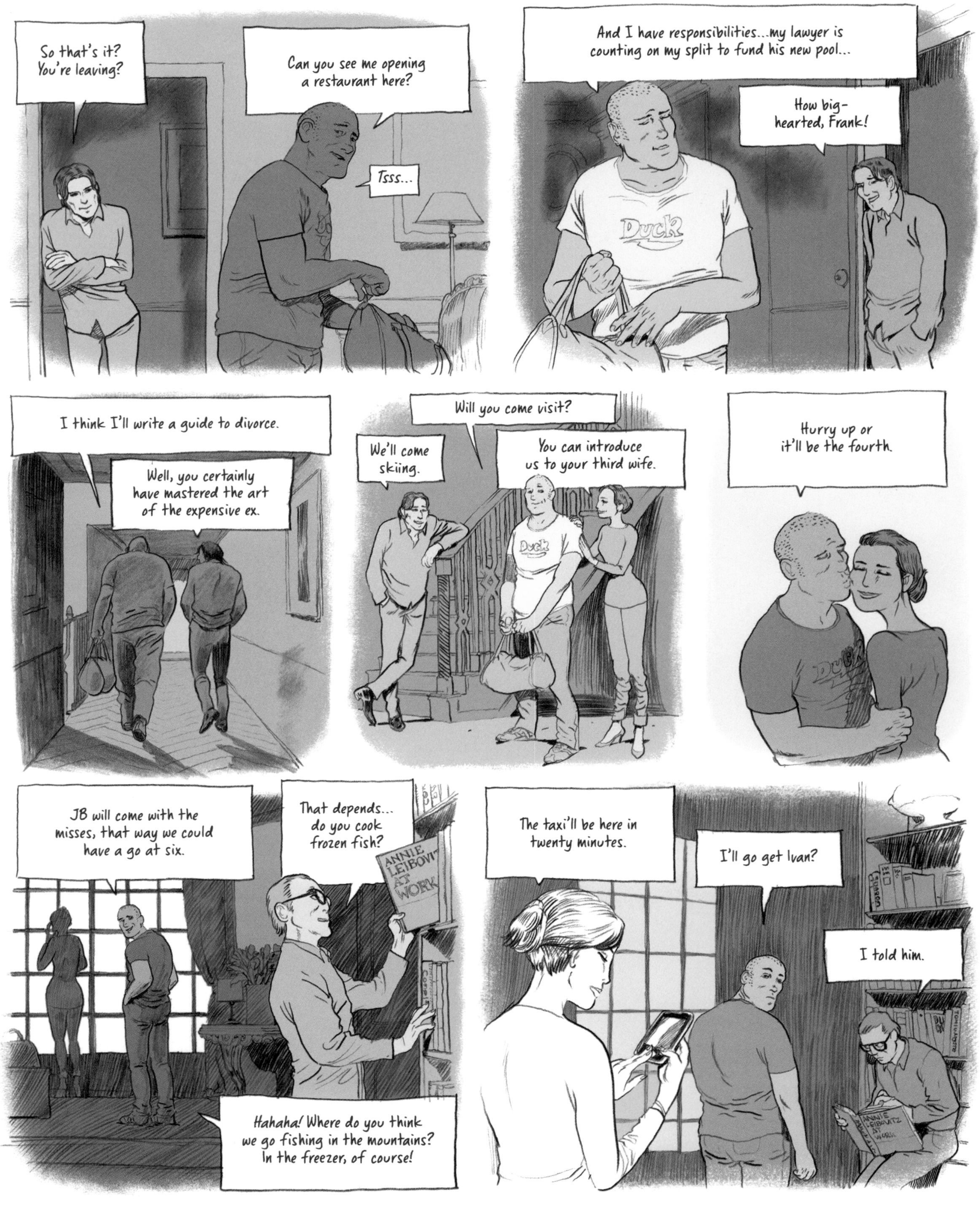
So that's it? You're leaving?
Can you see me opening a restaurant here?
Tsss...
And I have responsibilities...my lawyer is counting on my split to fund his new pool...
How big-hearted, Frank!
DUCK
I think I'll write a guide to divorce.
Well, you certainly have mastered the art of the expensive ex.
Will you come visit?
We'll come skiing.
You can introduce us to your third wife.
Hurry up or it'll be the fourth.
JB will come with the misses, that way we could have a go at six.
That depends... do you cook frozen fish?
Hahaha! Where do you think we go fishing in the mountains? In the freezer, of course!
The taxi'll be here in twenty minutes.
I'll go get Ivan?
I told him.

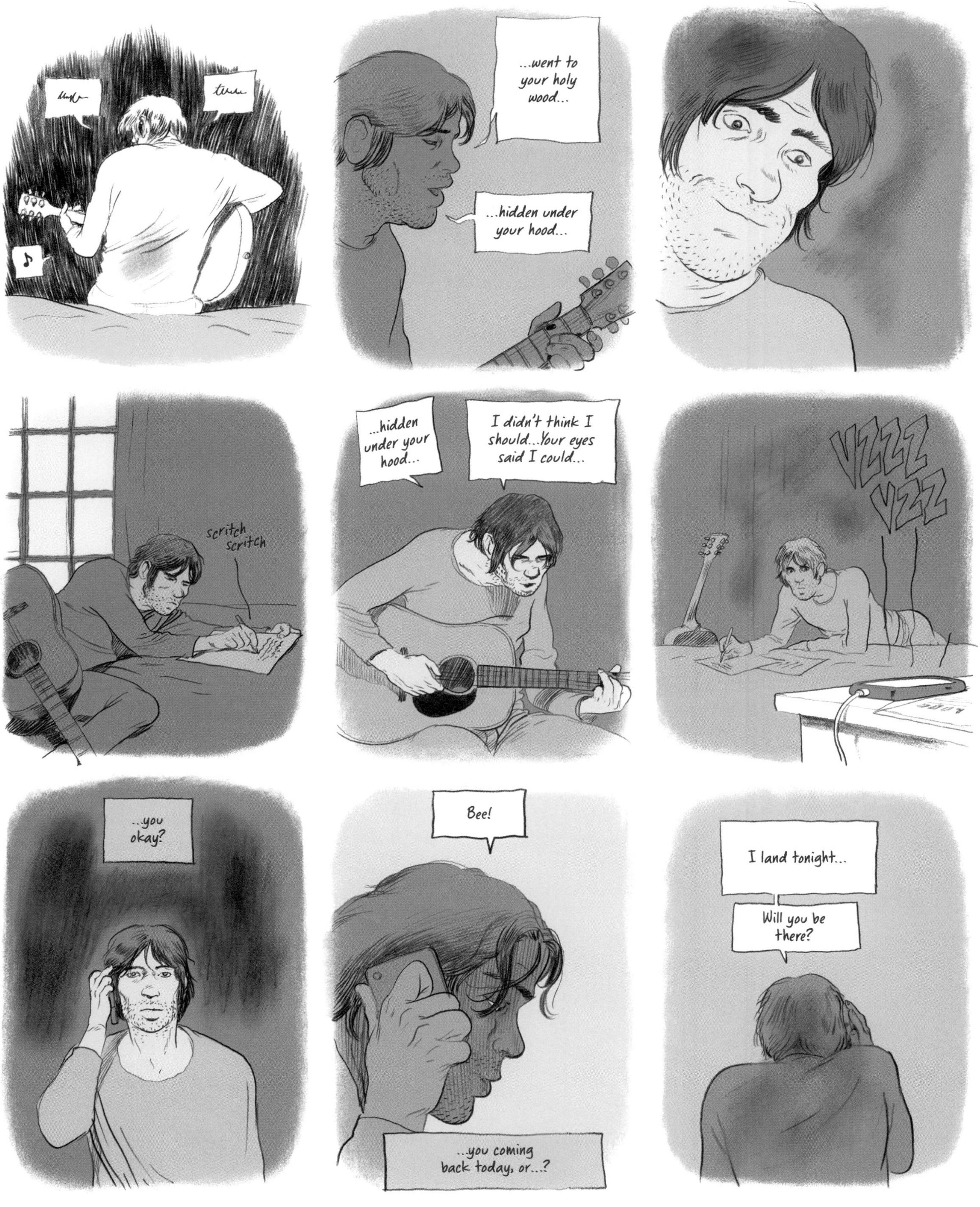

...went to your holy wood...
...hidden under your hood...
scritch scritch
...hidden under your hood...
I didn't think I should...Your eyes said I could...
VZZZ VZZ
..you okay?
Bee!
...you coming back today, or...?
I land tonight...
Will you be there?

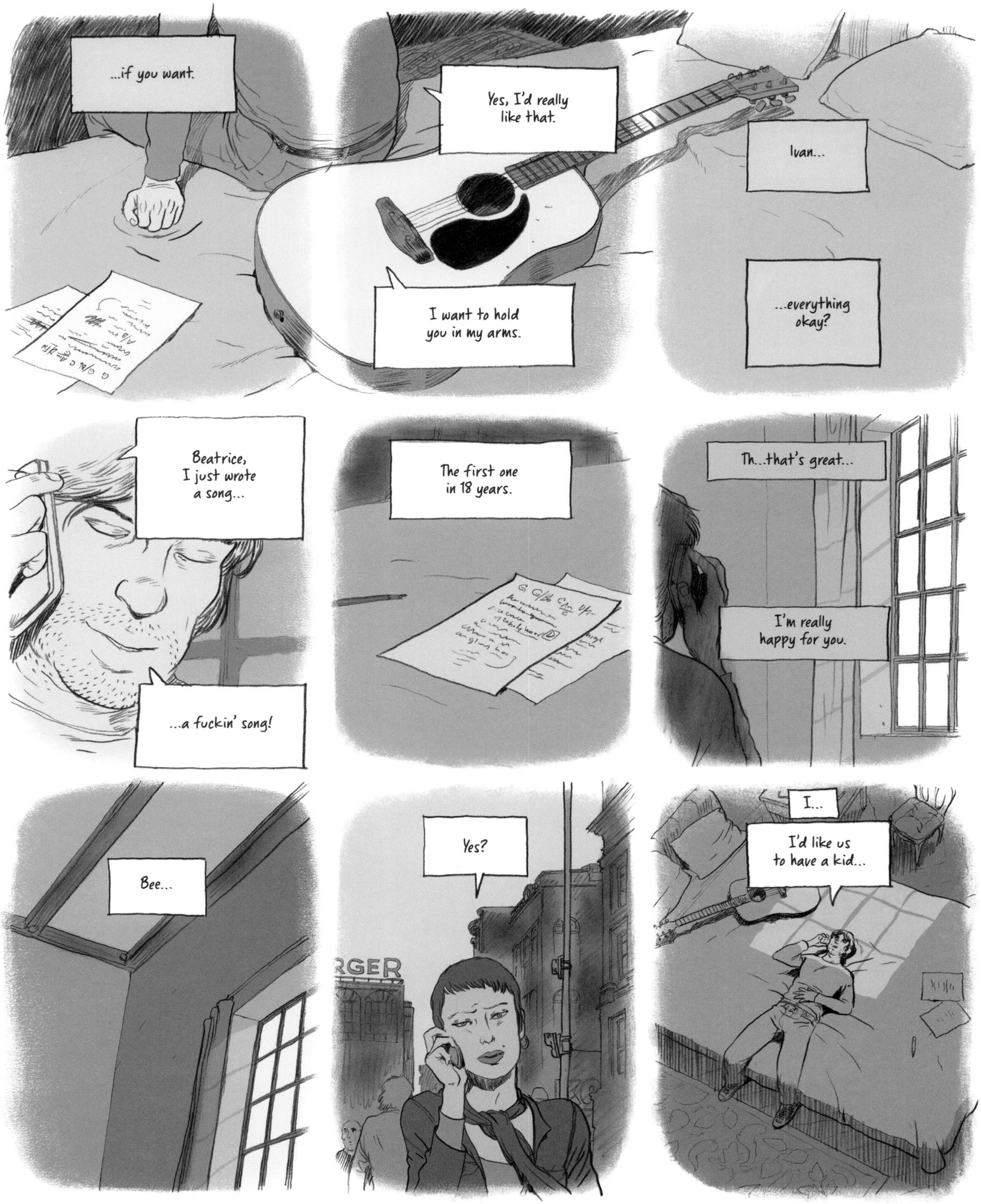
...if you want.
Yes, I'd really like that.
I want to hold you in my arms.
Ivan...
...everything okay?
Beatrice, I just wrote a song...
...a fuckin' song!
The first one in 18 years.
Th...that's great...
I'm really happy for you.
Bee...
Yes?
RGER
I...
I'd like us to have a kid...

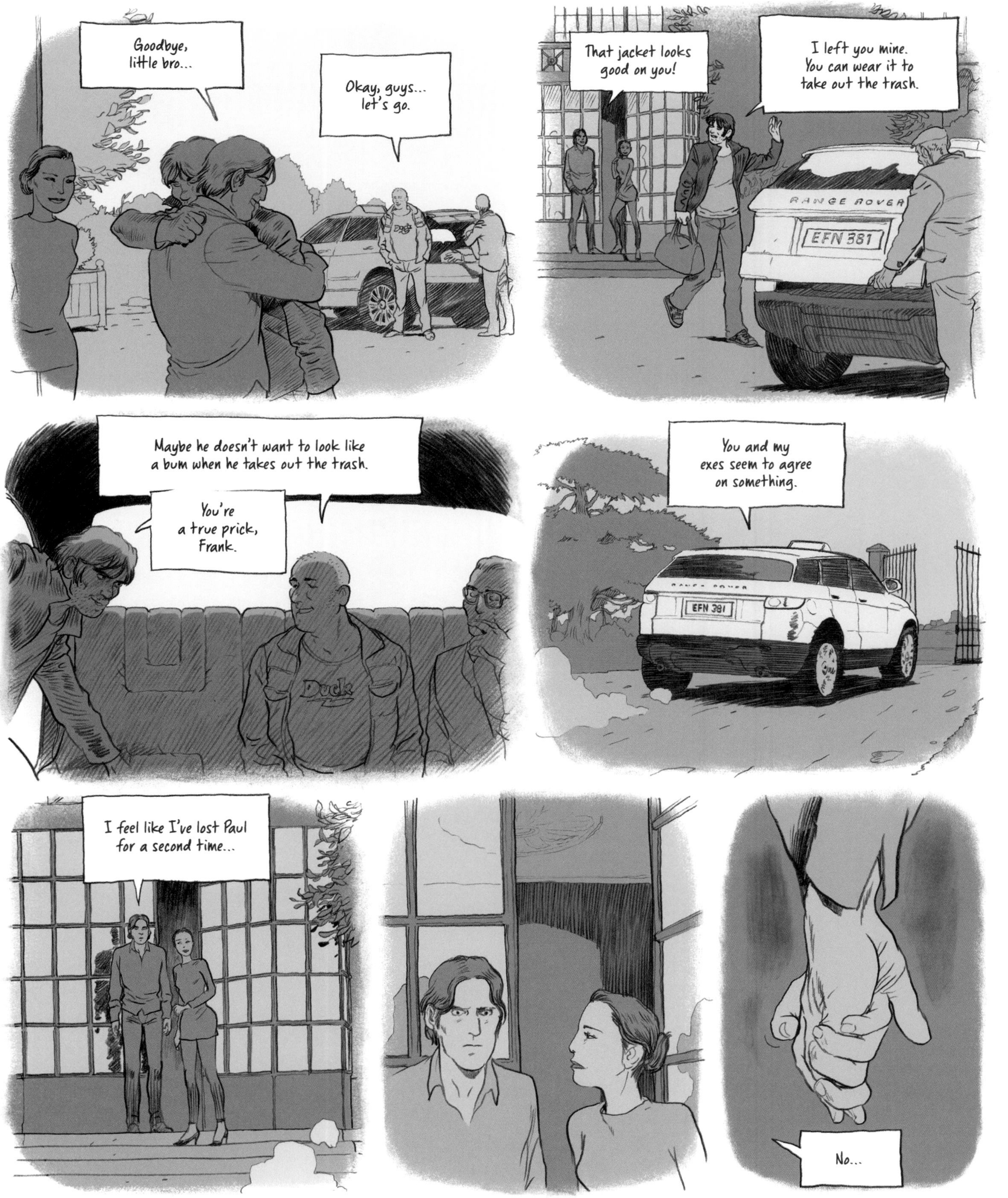
Goodbye, little bro...
Okay, guys... let's go.
That jacket looks good on you!
I left you mine. You can wear it to take out the trash.
RANGE ROVER
EFN 381
Maybe he doesn't want to look like a bum when he takes out the trash.
You're a true prick, Frank.
Duck
You and my exes seem to agree on something.
EFN 381
I feel like I've lost Paul for a second time...
No...

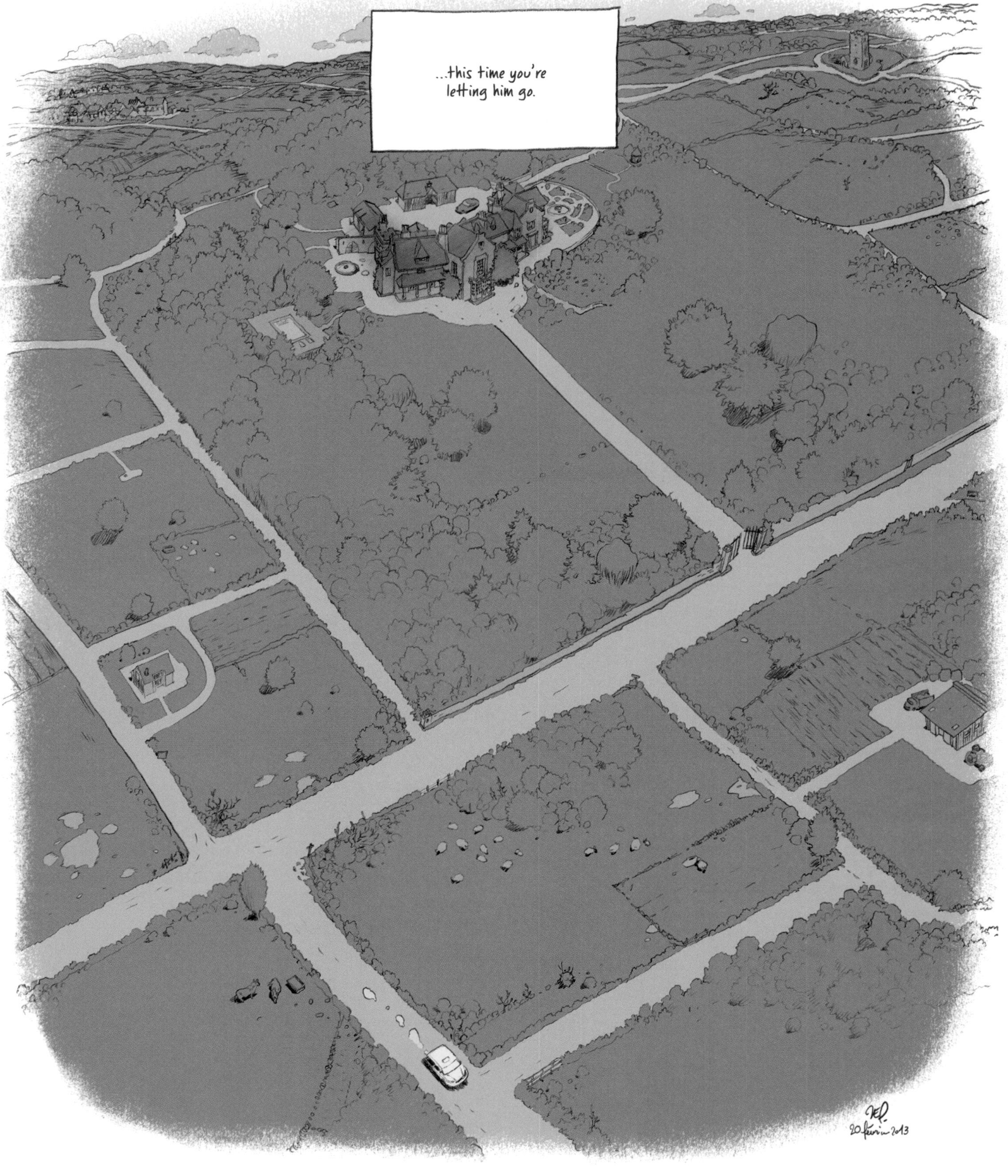
...this time you're letting him go.
20 février 2013

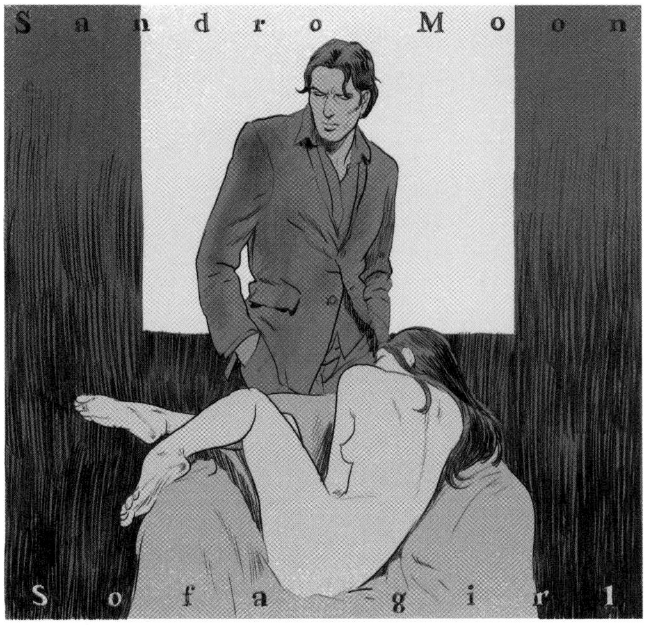
Sandro Moon
Sofagirl

A
STORY
OF MEN

ZEP